TO THE TEMPLE...

"Bring the one in," Citlallatonac's voice spoke from the temple, and they pushed him inside.

The first priest was sitting cross-legged on an ornamented block of stone before a statue of Coatlicue. In the half-light of the temple the goddess was hideously lifelike, glazed and painted and decorated with gems and gold plates. Her twin heads looked at him and her claw-handed arms appeared ready to seize.

"You have disobeyed the clan leaders," the first priest said loudly...Chimal came close, and when he did so he saw that the priest was older than he had thought. His hair, matted with blood and dirt and unwashed for years, had the desired frightening effect, as did the blood on his death-symboled robe...His skin had a waxy pallor except where patches of red powder had been dusted on his cheeks to simulate good health....

"You have disobeyed. Do you know the penalty?" The old man's voice cracked with rage.

"I did not disobey, therefore there is no penalty."

HARRY HARRISON

CAPTIVE UNIVERSE

ACE SCIENCE FICTION BOOKS
NEW YORK

CAPTIVE UNIVERSE

An Ace Science Fiction book / published by arrangement with
the author

PRINTING HISTORY
Berkley edition / February 1976
First Ace printing / December 1984

ISBN: 0-441-09142-3

Ace Science Fiction Books are published by
The Berkley Publishing Group,
200 Madison Avenue, New York, New York 10016.
PRINTED IN THE UNITED STATES OF AMERICA

THE VALLEY

1

O nen nontlacat
O nen nonqizaco
   ye nican in tlalticpac:
    Ninotolinia,
in manel nonquiz,
in manel nontlacat.
   ye nican in tlalticpac.

   In vain was I born,
   In vain was it written
    that here on earth:
     I suffer,
   Yet at least
  it was something
    to be born on earth.
           Aztec chant.

Chimal ran in panic. The moon was still hidden by the cliffs on the eastern side of the valley, but its light was already tipping their edges with silver. Once it had risen above them he would be as easily seen as the holy pyramid out here among the sprouting corn. Why had he not thought? Why had he taken the risk? His breath tore at his throat as he gasped and ran on, his heart pulsed like a great drum that filled his chest. Even the recent memory of Quiauh and her arms tight about him could not drive away the world-shaking fear—why had he done it?

If only he could reach the river, it was so close ahead. His woven sandals dug into the dry soil, pushing him forward toward the water and safety.

A sibilant, distant hissing cut through the silence of the night and Chimal's legs gave way, sending him to the ground in a spasm of terror. It was Coatlicue, she of the serpent heads, he was dead! He was dead!

Lying there, his fingers clawing uncontrollably at the

knee-high corn stalks, he struggled to put his thoughts in order, to speak his death chant because the time of dying had come. He had broken the rule, so he would die: a man cannot escape the gods. The hissing was louder now and it sliced through his head like a knife, he could not think, yet he must. With an effort he mumbled the first words of the chant as the moon rose above the ledge of rock, almost full, flooding the valley with glowing light and throwing a black shadow from every cornstalk about him. Chimal turned his head to look back over his shoulder and there, clear as the road to the temple, was the deep-dug line of his footprints between the rows of corn. Quiauh—they will find you!

He was guilty and for him there could be no escape. The taboo had been broken and Coatlicue the dreadful was coming for him. The guilt was his alone; he had forced his love on Quiauh, he had. Hadn't she struggled? It was written that the gods could be interceded with, and if they saw no evidence they would take him as a sacrifice and Quiauh might live. His knees were weak with terror yet he pulled himself to his feet and turned, running, starting back toward the village of Quilapa that he had so recently left, angling away from the revealing row of footprints.

Terror drove him on, though he knew escape was hopeless, and each time the hissing sliced the air it was closer until, suddenly, a larger shadow enveloped his shadow that fled before him and he fell. Fear paralyzed him and he had to fight against his own muscles to turn his head and see that which had pursued him.

"Coatlicue!" he screamed, driving all the air from his lungs with that single word.

High she stood, twice as tall as any man, and both her serpents' heads bent down toward him, eyes glowing redly with the lights of hell, forked tongues flicking in and out. As she circled about him the moonlight struck full onto her necklace of human hands and hearts, illuminated the skirt of writhing snakes that hung from her waist. As Coatlicue's twin mouths hissed the living kirtle moved, and the massed serpents hissed in echo. Chimal lay motionless, beyond terror now, accepting death from which there is no escape, spread-eagled like a sacrifice on the altar.

6

The goddess bent over him and he could see that she was just as she appeared in the stone carvings in the temple, fearful and inhuman, with claws instead of hands. They were not tiny pincers, like those of a scorpion or a river crayfish, but were great flat claws as long as his forearm that opened hungrily as they came at him. They closed, grating on the bones in his wrists, severing his right arm, then his left. Two more hands for that necklace.

"I have broken the law and left my village in the night and crossed the river. I die." His voice was only a whisper that grew stronger as he began the death chant in the shadow of the poised and waiting goddess.

I leave
Descend in one night to the underworld regions
Here we but meet
Briefly, transient on this earth . . .

When he had finished Coatlicue bent lower, reaching down past her writhing serpent kirtle, and tore out his beating heart.

2

Beside her, in a small pottery bowl set carefully in the shade of the house so they would not wilt, was a spray of quiauhxochitl, the rain flower after which she had been named. As she knelt over the stone metatl grinding corn, Quiauh murmured a prayer to the goddess of the flower asking her to keep the dark gods at bay. Today they drew so close to her she could scarcely breathe and only long habit enabled her to keep drawing the grinder back and forth over the slanted surface. Today was the sixteenth anniversary of *the* day, the day when they had found Chimal's body on this side of the riverbank, torn apart by Coatlicue's vengeance. Just two days after the Ripening Corn festival. Why had she been spared? Coatlicue must know that she had broken the taboo, just as Chimal had, yet she lived. Every year since then, on the anniversary of the day, she walked in fear. And each time death had passed her by. So far.

This year was the worst of all, because today they had

7

taken her son to the temple for judgment. Disaster must strike now. The gods had been watching all these years, waiting for this day, knowing all the time that her son Chimal was the son of Chimal-popoca, the man from Zaachila who had broken the clan taboo. She moaned deep in her throat when she breathed, yet she kept steadily grinding the fresh grains of corn.

The shadow of the valley wall was darkening her house and she had already patted out the tortillas between her palms and put them to bake on the cumal over the fire when she heard the slow footsteps. People had carefully avoided her house all day. She did not turn. It was someone coming to tell her that her son was a sacrifice, was dead. It was the priests coming to take her to the temple for her sin of sixteen years ago.

"My mother," the boy said. She saw him leaning weakly against the white wall of the house and when he moved his hand a red mark was left behind.

"Lie down here," she said, hurrying inside the house for a petlatl, then spreading this grass sleeping mat outside the door where there was still light. He was alive, they were both alive, the priests had simply beaten him! She stood, clasping her hands, wanting to sing, until he dropped face down on the mat and she saw that they had beaten his back too, as well as his arms. He lay there quietly, eyes open and staring across the valley, while she mixed water with the healing herbs and patted them onto the bloody weals: he shivered slightly at the touch, but said nothing.

"Can you tell your mother why this happened?" she asked, looking at his immobile profile and trying to read some meaning into his face. She could not tell what he was thinking. It had always been this way since he had been a little boy. His thoughts seemed to go beyond her, to leave her out. This must be part of a curse: if one broke a taboo one must suffer.

"It was a mistake."

"The priests do not make mistakes or beat a boy for a mistake."

"They did this time. I was climbing the cliff . . ."

"Then it was no mistake that they beat you—it is forbidden to climb the cliff."

"No, mother," he said patiently, "it is not forbidden to climb the cliff—it is forbidden to climb the cliff to attempt

8

to leave the valley, that is the law as Tezcatlipoca said it. But it is also permitted to climb the cliffs to the height of three men to take birds' eggs, or for other important reasons. I was only two men high on the cliff and I was after birds' eggs. That is the law."

"If—that is the law, why were you beaten?" She sat back on her heels, frowning in concentration.

"They did not remember the law and did not agree with me and they had to look it up in the book which took a long time—and when they did they found *I* was right and they were wrong." He smiled, coldly. It was not a boy's smile at all. "So then they beat me because I had argued with priests and set myself above them."

"As so they should have." She rose and poured some water from the jug to rinse her hands. "You must learn your place. You must not argue with priests."

For almost all of his life Chimal had been hearing this, or words like it, and had long since learned that the best answer was no answer. Even when he worked hard to explain his thoughts and feelings his mother never understood. It was far better to keep these thoughts to himself.

Particularly since he had lied to everyone. He had been trying to climb the cliff; the birds' eggs were just a ready excuse in case he were discovered.

"Stay here and eat," Quiauh said, putting a child's evening portion of two tortillas before him, dry, flat corncakes over a foot wide. "I will make atolli while you eat these."

Chimal sprinkled salt on the tortilla and tore off a piece which he chewed on slowly, watching his mother through the open door of the house as she bent over the fire stones and stirred the pot. She was at ease now, the fear and the beating finished and forgotten, her typical Aztec features relaxed, with the firelight glinting from her golden hair and blue eyes. He felt very close to her; they had been alone in this house since his father had died when Chimal had been very young. Yet at the same time he felt so distant. He could explain nothing to her about the things that troubled him.

He sat up to eat the atolli when his mother brought it to him, spooning up the corn gruel with a piece of tortilla. It was rich and filling, deliciously flavored with honey and hot chillies. His back was feeling better as were his arms:

the bleeding had stopped where the skin had been broken by the whipping stick. He drank cool water from the small pot and looked up at the darkening sky. Above the cliffs, to the west, the sky was red as fire and against it soared the zopilote vultures, black silhouettes that vanished and reappeared. He watched until the light faded from the sky and they were gone. That was the spot where he started to climb the cliff; they were the reason he had climbed it.

The stars were out, sharp and sparkling in the clear air, while inside the house the familiar work noises had ceased. There was just a rustle as his mother unrolled her petlatl on the sleeping platform, then she called to him.

"It is time to sleep."

"I'll sleep here for awhile, the air is cool on my back."

Her voice was troubled. "It is not right to sleep outside, everyone sleeps inside."

"Just for a little while, no one can see me, then I will come in."

She was silent after that but he lay on his side and watched the stars rise and wheel overhead and sleep would not come. The village was quiet and everyone was asleep and he thought again about the vultures.

He went over his plan once more, step by step, and could find no fault in it. Or rather one fault only—that a priest had happened to pass and had seen him. The rest of the plan had been perfect, even the law which permitted him to climb the wall had been as he remembered it. And the vultures *did* fly to the same spot on the cliff above. Day after day, and for as long as he remembered this had interested him and he had wanted to know why. It had bothered and annoyed him that he did not know the reason, until finally he had made his plan. After all—was not the vulture the totem of his clan? He had a right to know all that there was to know about them. No one else cared about it, that was certain. He had asked different people and most of them had not bothered to answer, just pushing him away when he persisted. Or if they had answered they had just shrugged or laughed and said that was the way vultures were and forgotten about it at once. They didn't care, none of them cared at all. Not the children, especially the children, nor the adults or even the priests. But he cared.

He had had other questions, but he had stopped asking

questions about things many years ago. Because unless the questions had simple answers that the people knew, or there were answers from the holy books that the priests knew, asking just made people angry. Then they would shout at him or even hit him, even though children were rarely struck, and it did not take Chimal long to discover that this was because they themselves did not know. Therefore he had to look for answers in his own way, like this matter with the vultures.

It had bothered him because although much was known about the vultures, there was one thing that was not known—or even thought about. Vultures ate carrion, everyone knew that, and he himself had seen them tearing at the carcasses of armadillos and birds. They nested in the sand, laid their eggs, raised their scruffy chicks here. That was all they did, there was nothing else to know about them.

Except—why did they always fly to that one certain spot on the cliff? His anger at not knowing, and at the people who would not help him or even listen to him, was rubbed raw by the pain of his recent whipping. He could not sleep or even sit still. He stood up, invisible in the darkness, opening and closing his fists. Then, almost without volition, he moved silently away from his home, threading his way through the sleeping houses of the village of Quilapa. Even though people did not walk about at night. It was not a taboo, just something that was not done. He did not care and felt bold in doing it. At the edge of the open desert he stopped, looked at the dark barrier of the cliffs and shivered. Should he go there now—and climb? Did he dare to do at night what he had been prevented from doing during the day? His feet answered for him, carrying him forward. It would certainly be easy enough since he had marked a fissure that seemed to run most of the way up to the ledge where the vultures sat. The mesquite tore at his legs when he left the path and made his way through the clumps of tall cacti. When he reached the field of maguey plants the going was easier, and he walked straight forward between their even rows until he reached the base of the cliff.

Only when he was there did he admit how afraid he was. He looked around carefully, but there was no one else to be seen and he had not been followed. The night

11

air was cool on his body and he shivered: his arms and back still hurt. There would be bigger trouble if he were found climbing the cliff again, worse than a beating this time. He shivered harder and wrapped his arms about himself and was ashamed of his weakness. Quickly, before he could worry anymore and find a reason to turn back, he leaped against the rock until his fingers caught in the horizontal crack, then pulled himself up.

Once he was moving it was easier, he had to concentrate on finding the hand and toe holds he had used that morning and there was little time for thought. He passed the bird's nest that he had raided and felt his only qualm. Now he was certainly higher than three men above the ground—but he was not trying to climb to the top of the cliff, so he could not really be said to be breaking the law. . . . A piece of rock gave way under his fingers and he almost fell, his worries were instantly forgotten in the spurt of fear as he scrabbled for a new hold. He climbed higher.

Just below the ledge Chimal stopped to rest with his toes wedged into a crack. There was an overhang above him and there seemed to be no way around it. Searching the blackness of stone against the stars his glance went over the valley and he shuddered and pressed himself against the cliff: he had not realized before how high he had climbed. Stretching away below was the dark floor of the valley with his village of Quilapa, then the deep cut of the river beyond. He could even make out the other village of Zaachila and the far wall of the canyon. This was taboo—Coatlicue walked the river at night and the sight alone of her twin serpent heads would instantly kill you and send you to the underworld. He shuddered and turned his face to the stone. Hard rock, cold air, space all around him, loneliness that possessed him.

There was no way to know how long he hung like that, some minutes surely because his toes were numb where they were wedged into the crevice. All he wanted to do now was to return safely to the ground, so impossibly distant below, and only the wavering flame of his anger kept him from doing this. He would go down, but first he would see how far the overhang ran. If he could not pass it he would have to return, and he would have done his best to reach the ledge. Working his way around a rough spire he saw that the overhang did run the length of the

12

ledge—but an immense bite had been taken from the lip. At some time in the past a falling boulder must have shattered it. There was a way up. With scratching fingers he hauled himself up the slope until his head came above the level of the ledge.

Something black hurtled at him, buffeting his head, washing him in a foul and dusty smell. A spasm of unreasoning fear clamped his hands onto the rock or he would have fallen, then the blackness was gone and a great vulture flapped his way unsteadily out into the darkness. Chimal laughed out loud. There was nothing here to be frightened of, he had reached the right spot and had disturbed the bird that must have been perched up here, that was all. He pulled himself onto the ledge and stood up. The moon would be rising soon, and was already glowing on a high band of clouds in the east, lighting the sky and blotting out the stars there. The ledge was clear before him, empty of any other vultures, although it was foul with their droppings. There was little else here of any interest, other than the black opening of a cave in the rising wall of rock before him. He shuffled toward it, but there was nothing to be seen in the blackness of its depths: he stopped at the dark entrance and could force himself to go no further. What could possibly be in it? It would not be long before the moon rose and he might see better then. He would wait.

It was cold this high up, exposed to the wind, but he took no notice. The sky was growing lighter every moment and grayness seeped into the cave, further and further from the entrance. When at last the moonlight shone full into it he felt betrayed. There was nothing here to see. The cave wasn't a cave after all, just a deep gouge in the face of the cliff that ended no more than two men's lengths inside the opening. There was just rock, solid rock, with what appeared to be more rocks on the stony floor. He pushed his foot at the nearest one and it moved squashily away from him. This was no rock—what could it possibly be? He bent to pick it up and his fingers told him what it was at the same instant his nose identified it.

Meat.

Horror drove him back and almost over the edge to his death. He stopped, at the very brink, trembling and wiping his hand over and over again on the stone and gravel.

Meat. Flesh. And he had actually touched it, a piece over a foot, almost two feet in length, and as thick as his hand was long. On feast days, he had eaten meat and had watched his mother prepare it. Fish, or small birds caught in a net, or the best of all, guajolote, the turkey with the sweet white meat, cooked in strips and laid on the mashed beans and tortillas. But how big was the biggest piece of meat from the biggest bird? There was only one creature from which pieces of flesh this big could have been wrenched.

Man.

It was a wonder he did not keep going to his death when he slid over the edge of the cliff, but his young fingers caught of their own accord and his toes dug in and he climbed downward. He had no memory of the descent. The stream of his thoughts broke into drops like water when he remembered what he had seen. Meat, men, sacrifices the zopilote god had placed here for the vultures to eat. He had seen it. Would his body be chosen next to feed them? Trembling uncontrollably when he reached the bottom, he fell and long moments passed before he could force himself up from the sand to stumble back toward the village. Physical exhaustion brought some relief from the terror and he began to realize how dangerous it would be if he were discovered now, coming back this way. He crept cautiously between the brown houses, with their windows like dark, staring eyes, until he reached his own home. His petlatl was still lying where he had left it; it seemed incredible that nothing should have changed in the endless time that he had been away, and he gathered it up and pulled it after him through the doorway and spread it near the banked but still warm fire. When he pulled the blanket over himself he fell asleep instantly, anxious to leave the waking world that had suddenly become more frightening than the worst nightmare.

3

*The number of the months is eighteen, and
the name of the eighteenmonths is a year.
The third month is Tozoztontli and this is
when the corn is planted and there are
prayers and fasting so that the rain will
come so that in the seventh month the corn
will ripen. Then in the eighth month
prayers are said to keep away the rain that
would destroy the ripening corn . . .*

The rain god, Tlaloc, was being very difficult this year. He
was always a moody god, with good reason perhaps, because so much was asked of him. In certain months rain
was desperately needed to water the young corn, but in
other months clear skies and sunlight were necessary to
ripen it. Therefore, in many years, Tlaloc did not bring
rain, or brought too much, and the crop was small and the
people went hungry.

Now he was not listening at all. The sun burned in a
cloudless sky and one hot day followed another without
change. Lacking water, the small shoots of new corn that
pressed up through the hardened and cracked earth were
far smaller than they should have been, and had a gray
and tired look to them. Between the rows of stunted corn
almost the entire village of Quilapa stamped and wailed,
while the priest shouted his prayer and the cloud of dust
rose high in the stifling air.

Chimal did not find it easy to cry. Almost all of the
others had tears streaking furrows into their dust-covered
cheeks, tears to touch the rain god's heart so that his tears
of rain would fall as theirs did. As a child Chimal had
never taken part in this ceremony, but now that he had
passed his twentieth year he was an adult, and shared
adult duties and responsibilities. He shuffled his feet on
the hard dirt and thought of the hunger that would come
and the pain in his belly, but this made him angry instead
of tearful. Rubbing at his eyes only made them hurt. In

the end he moistened his finger with saliva, when no one was looking, and drew the lines in the dust on his face.

Of course the women cried the best, wailing and tearing at their braided hair until it came loose and hung in lank yellow strands about their shoulders. When their tears slowed or stopped, the men beat them with straw-filled bags.

Someone brushed against Chimal's leg, pressing a warm and yielding flank against him. He moved further down the row, but a moment later the pressure had returned. It was Malinche, a girl with a round face, round eyes, a round figure. She stared, wide-eyed, up at him while she cried. Her mouth was open so he could see the black gap in the white row of her upper teeth, she had bit on a stone in her beans and broke it when she was a child, and her eyes streamed and her nose ran with the intensity of her emotions. She was still almost a child, but she had turned sixteen and was therefore a woman. In sudden rage he began to beat her about the shoulders and back with his bag. She did not pull away, or appear to notice it at all, while her tear-filled round eyes still stared at him, as pale blue and empty of warmth as the winter sky.

Old Atototl passed in the next row, carrying a plump eating dog to the priest. Since he was the cacique, the leading man in Quilapa, this was his privilege. Chimal pushed his way into the crowd as they all turned to follow. At the edge of the field Citlallatonac waited, a fearful sight in his filthy black robe, spattered all over with blood, and thick with embroidered skulls and bones along the bottom edge where it trailed in the dust. Atototl came up to him, arms extended, and the two old men bent over the wriggling puppy. It looked up at them, its tongue out and panting in the heat, while Citlallatonac, as first priest this was his duty, plunged his black obsidian knife into the little animal's chest. Then, with practiced skill, he tore out its still beating heart and held it high as sacrifice to Tlaloc, letting the blood spatter among the stalks of corn.

There was nothing more then that could be done. Yet the sky was still a cloudless bowl of heat. By ones and twos the villagers straggled unhappily from the fields and Chimal, who always walked alone, was not surprised to find Malinche beside him. She placed her feet down heavily and walked in silence, but only for a short while.

16

"Now the rains will come," she said with bland assurance. "We have wept and prayed and the priest has sacrificed."

But we always weep and pray, he thought, and the rains come or do not come. And the priests in the temple will eat well tonight, good fat dog. Aloud he said, "The rains will come."

"I am sixteen," she said, and when he did not answer she added, "I make good tortillas and I am strong. The other day we had no masa and the corn was not husked and there was even no lime water to make the masa to make the tortillas, so my mother said . . ."

Chimal was not listening. He stayed inside himself and let the sound of her voice go by him like the wind, with as much effect. They walked on together toward the village. Something moved above, drifting out of the glare of the sun and sliding across the sky toward the gray wall of the western cliffs beyond the houses. His eyes followed it, a zopilote going toward that ledge on the cliff . . . Though his eyes stayed upon the soaring bird his mind slithered away from it. The cliff was not important nor were the birds important: they meant nothing to him. Some things did not bear thinking about. His face was grim and unmoving as they walked on, yet in his thoughts was a twist of hot irritation. The sight of the bird and the memory of the cliff that night—it could be forgotten but not with Malinche's prying away at him. "I like tortillas," he said when he became aware that the voice had stopped.

"The way I like to eat them best . . ." the voice started up again, spurred by his interest, and he ignored it. But the little arrowhead of annoyance in his head did not go away, even when he turned and left Malinche suddenly and went into his house. His mother was at the metatl, grinding the corn for the evening meal; it would take two hours to prepare it. And another two hours of the same labor for the morning meal. This was a woman's work. She looked up and nodded at him without slowing the back and forth motion.

"I see Malinche out there. She is a good girl and works very hard."

Malinche was framed by the open entranceway, legs wide, bare feet planted firmly in the dust, the roundness of her large breasts pushing out the huipil draped across her

17

shoulders, her arms at her side and her fists clenched as though waiting for something. Chimal turned away and, squatting on the mat, drank cool water from the porous jug.

"You are almost twenty-one years of age, my son," Quiauh said with irritating calmness, "and the clans must be joined."

Chimal knew all this, but he did not wish to accept it. At 21 a man must marry; at 16 a girl must marry. A woman needed a man to raise the food for her; a man needed a woman to prepare the food for him. The clan leaders would decide who would be married in such a way that it profited the clans the most, and the matchmaker would be called in . . .

"I will see if I can get some fish," he said suddenly, standing and taking his knife from the niche in the wall. His mother said nothing, her lowered head bobbed as she bent over her work. Malinche was gone and he hurried between the houses to the path that led south, through the cactus and rock, toward the end of the valley. It was still very hot and when the path went along the rim of the ravine he could see the river below, dried to a sluggish trickle this time of year. Yet it was still water and it looked cool. He hurried toward the dusty green of the trees at the head of the valley, the almost vertical walls of stone closing in on each side as he went forward. It was cooler here on the path under the trees: one of them had fallen since he had been here last, he would have to bring back some firewood.

Then he reached the pond below the cliffs and his eyes went up along the thin stream of the waterfall that dropped down from high above. It splattered into the pond which, although it was smaller now with a wide belt of mud around it, he knew was still deep at the center. There would be fish out there, big fish with sweet meat on their bones, lurking under the rocks along the edge. With his knife he cut a long, thin branch and began to fashion a fish spear.

Lying on his stomach on a shelf of rock that overhung the pool he looked deep into its transparent depths. There was a flicker of silver motion as a fish moved into the shadows: it was well out of reach. The air was dry and hot, the distant hammer of a bird's bill on wood sounded

18

unnaturally loud in the silence. Zopilotes were birds and they fed on all kinds of meat, even human meat, he had seen that for himself. When? Five or six years ago?

As always, his thoughts started to veer away from that memory—but this time they did not succeed. The hot dart of irritation that had been planted in the field still stirred at his mind and, in sudden anger, he clutched at the memory of that night. What *had* he seen? Pieces of meat. Armadillo, or rabbit perhaps? No, he could not trick himself into believing that. Man was the only creature who was big enough to have furnished those lumps of flesh. One of the gods had put them there, Mixtec perhaps, the god of death, to feed his servants the vultures who look after the dead. Chimal had seen the god's offering and had fled—and nothing had happened. Since that night he had walked in silence waiting for the vengeance that had never arrived.

Where had the years gone? What had happened to the boy who was always in trouble, always asking questions that had no answers? The prod of irritation struck deep and Chimal stirred on the rock, then rolled over and looked up at the sky where a vulture, like the black mark of an omen, soared silently out of sight above the valley's wall. I was the boy, Chimal said, almost speaking aloud, and admitting to himself for the first time what had happened, and I was so filled with fear that I went inside myself and sealed myself in tightly like a fish sealed in mud for baking. Why does this bother me now?

With a quick spring he was on his feet, looking around as though for something to kill. Now he was a man and people would no longer leave him alone as they had when he was a boy. He would have responsibilities, he must do new things. He must take a wife and build a house and have a family and grow old and in the end . . .

"*No!*" he shouted as loudly as he could and sprang far out from the rock. The water, cool from the melting snows of the mountains, wrapped around and pressed onto him and he sank deep. His open eyes saw the shadowed blueness that surrounded him and the wrinkled, light-shot surface of the water above. It was another world here and he wanted to remain in it, away from his world. He swam lower until his ears hurt and his hands plunged deep into the mud on the pool's bottom. But then, even while he was

19

thinking that he would remain here, his chest burned and his hands of their own thinking sent him arrowing back to the surface. His mouth opened, without his commanding it to, and he breathed in a great chestful of soothing air.

Climbing out of the pool he stood at the edge, water streaming from his loincloth and seeping from his sandals, and looked up at the wall of rock and the falling water. He could not stay forever in that world beneath the water. And then, with a sudden burst of understanding, he realized that he also could not stay in this world that was his valley. If he were a bird he could fly away! There had been a way out of the valley once, those must have been wonderful days, but the earthquake had ended that. In his mind's eye he could see the swamp at the other end of the long valley, pressed up against the base of that immense rubble of rock and boulders that sealed the exit. The water seeped slowly out between the rocks and the birds soared above, but for the people of the valley there was no way out. They were sealed in by the great, overhanging boulders and by the curse that was even harder to surmount. It was Omeyocan's curse, and he is the god whose name is never spoken aloud, only whispered lest he overhear. It was said that the people had forgotten the gods, the temple had been dusty and the sacrificial altar dry. Then, in one day and one night, Omeyocan had shaken the hills until they fell and sealed this valley off from the rest of the world for five times a hundred years at which time, if the people had served the temple well, the exit would be opened once again. The priests never said how much time had passed, and it did not matter. The penance would not end in their lifetimes.

What was the outside world like? There were mountains in it, that he knew. He could see their distant peaks and the snow that whitened them in winter and shrank to small patches on their north flanks in the summer. Other than that he had no idea. There must be villages, like his, that he could be sure of. But what else? They must know things that his people did not know, such as where to find metal and what to do with it. There were still some treasured axes and corn knives in the valley made from a shining substance called iron. They were softer than the obsidian tools, but did not break and could be sharpened over and over again. And the priests had a box made of this iron set with brilliant jewels which they showed on special festival days.

How he wanted to see the world that had produced these things! If he could leave he would—if only there were a way—and even the gods would not be able to stop him. Yet, even as he thought this he bent, raising his arm, waiting for the blow.

The gods would stop him. Coatlicue still walked and punished and he had seen the handless victims of her justice. There was no escape.

He was numb again, which was good. If you did not feel you could not be hurt. His knife was on the rock where he had left it and he remembered to pick it up because it had cost him many hours of hard work to shape the blade. But the fish were forgotten, as was the firewood: he brushed by the dead tree without seeing it. His feet found the trail and in welcome numbness he started back through the trees to the village.

When the trail followed the dried up river bed he could see the temple and the school on the far bank. A boy, he was from the other village of Zaachila and Chimal did not know his name, was waving from the edge, calling something through his cupped hands. Chimal stopped to listen.

"Temple . . ." he shouted, and something that sounded like *Tezcatlipoca,* which Chimal hoped it was not since the Lord of Heaven and Earth, inflicter and healer of frightful diseases, was not a name to be spoken lightly. The boy, realizing that he could not be heard, clambered down the far bank and splashed through the thin stream of water in the center. He was panting when he climbed up next to Chimal, but his eyes were wide with excitement.

"Popoca, do you know him, he is a boy from our village?" He rushed on without waiting for an answer. "He has seen visions and talked about them to others and the priests have heard the talk and have seen him and they have said that . . . Tezcatlipoca," excited as he was he stumbled over speaking that name aloud, ". . . has possessed him. They have taken him to the pyramid temple."

"Why?" Chimal asked, and knew the answer before it was spoken.

"Citlallatonac will free the god."

They must go there, of course, since everyone was expected to attend a ceremony as important as this one. Chimal did not wish to see it but he made no protest since it was his duty to be there. He left the boy when they reached the village and went to his home, but his mother had already gone as had almost everyone else. He put his knife away and set out on the well trodden path down the valley to the temple. The crowd was gathered, silently, at the temple base, but he could see clearly even where he stood to the rear. On a ledge above was the carved stone block, cut through with holes and stained by the accumulated blood of countless years. A youth was being tied, unprotesting, to the top of the block, and his bindings secured by passing through the holes in the stone. One of the priests stood over him and blew through a paper cone and, for an instant, a white cloud enveloped the young man's face. Yauhtli, the powder from the root of the plant, that made men asleep when they were awake and numbed them to pain. By the time Citlallatonac appeared the lesser priests had shaved the boy's head so the ritual could begin. The first priest himself carried the bowl of tools that he would need. A shudder passed through the youth's body, although he did not cry out, when the flap of skin was cut from his skull and the procedure began.

There was a movement among the people as the rotating arrowhead drilled into the bone of the skull and, without volition, Chimal found himself standing in the first rank. The details were painfully clear from here as first priest drilled a series of holes in the bone, joined them—then levered up and removed the freed disk of bone.

"You may come forth now, Tezcatlipoca," the priest said, and absolute silence fell over the crowd as this dread name was spoken. "Speak now, Popoca," he told the boy. "What is it that you saw?" As he said this the priest pressed with the arrowhead again at the shining gray tissue inside the wound. The boy replied with a low moan and his lips moved.

"Cactus . . . in the high bed against the wall . . . picking the fruit and it was late, but I was not finished . . . Even if the sun went down I would be in the village by dark . . . I turned and saw it . . ."

"Come forth, Tezcatlipoca, here is the way," the first priest said, and pushed his knife deep into the wound.

22

"SAW THE LIGHT OF THE GODS COME TO-
WARD ME AS THE SUN WENT . . ." the youth
screamed, then arched up once against his restraining
bonds and was still.

"Tezcatlipoca has gone," Citlallatonac said, dropping
his instruments into the bowl, "and the boy is free."

Dead also, Chimal thought, and turned away.

4

It was cooler now as evening approached, and the sun was
not as strong on Chimal's back as it had been earlier. Ever
since leaving the temple he had squatted here in the white
sand of the riverbed staring into the narrow trickle of stagnant water. At first he had not known what had brought
him here and then, when he had realized what was driving
him, fear had kept him pinned to this spot. This day had
been distrubing in every way and Popoca's sacrificial
death had heated the ferment of his thoughts to a boil.
What had the boy seen? Could he see it too? Would he die
if he saw it?

When he stood his legs almost folded under him, he had
been seated in the squat position so long, and instead of
jumping the stream he splashed through it. He had wanted
to die earlier under the water, but he had not, so what difference did it make if he died now? Life here was—what
was the right word for it?—unbearable. The thought of
the unchanging endlessness of the days ahead of him
seemed far worse than the simple act of dying. The boy
had seen something, the gods had possessed him for seeing
it, and the priests had killed him for seeing it. What could
be so important? He could not imagine—and it made no
difference. Anything new in this valley of unchange was
something that he had to experience.

By staying close to the swamp at the north end of the
valley he remained unseen, circling the corn and maguey
fields that encircled Zaachila. This was unwanted land,
just cactus, mesquite and sand, and no one saw him pass.
The shadows were stretching their purple lengths along the
ground now and he hurried to be at the eastern wall of the

cliff beyond Zaachila before the sun set. What had the boy seen?

There was only one bed of fruit-bearing cactus that fitted the description, the one at the top of a long slope of broken rubble and sand. Chimal knew where it was and when he reached it the sun was just dropping behind the distant peaks of the mountains. He scrambled up on all fours to the top of the slope, to the cactus, then clambered to the summit of a large boulder. Height might have something to do with what Popoca had seen, the higher the better. From his vantage point the entire valley opened out, with the village of Zaachila before him, then the dark slash of the riverbed and his own village beyond that. A projecting turn of the cliffs hid the waterfall at the south end of the valley, but the swamp and the giant stones that sealed it to the north were clearly visible, though darkening now as the sun slipped from sight. While he watched it vanished behind the mountains. That was all. Nothing. The sky went from red to a deeper purple and he was about to climb down from his vantage point.

When the beam of golden light spun out at him.

It lasted only an instant. If he had not been looking intently in the right direction he would never have seen it. A golden thread, thin as a slice of fire, that stretched across the sky from the direction of the vanished sun directly toward him, bright as the reflection of light upon the water. But there was no water there, just sky. What had it been?

With a sudden start that shook his body he realized where he was—and how late it was. The first stars were coming out above him and he was far from the village and his side of the river.

Coatlicue!

Ignoring anything else he hurled himself from the boulder and sprawled in the sand, then came up running. It was almost dark and everyone would be bent over the evening meal: he headed directly toward the river. Fear drove him on, around the bunched darkness of the cactus and over the low, thorny shrubs. *Coatlicue!* She was no myth: he had seen her victims. Reason fled and he ran like an animal pursued.

When he reached the bank of the riverbed it was completely dark and he had only the light of the stars to show him the way. It was even darker below the bank—and this was where Coatlicue dwelled. Trembling, he hesitated, unable to force himself down into the deeper blackness below.

And then, far off to his right in the direction of the swamp, he heard the hissing as of a giant snake. It was she!

Hesitating no longer he threw himself forward, rolled over and over on the soft sand and splashed through the water. The hissing came again. Was it louder? Tearing with desperate fingers he climbed the far bank and, sobbing for air, ran on through the fields, not stopping until a solid wall loomed up before him. He collapsed against the side of the first building, clutching the rough adobe bricks with his fingers and sprawling there, gasping, knowing he was safe. Coatlicue would not come here.

When his breathing was normal again he stood and made his way silently between the houses until he came to his home. His mother was turning tortillas on the cumal and she looked up when he came in.

"You are very late."

"I was at another house."

He sat and reached for the water bottle, then changed his mind and took the container of octli instead. The fermented juice of the maguey could bring drunkenness, but happiness and peace as well. As a man he could drink it when he wanted to and was still not used to this liberty. His mother looked at him out of the corners of her eyes but said nothing. He took a very long drink, then had to fight hard to control the coughing that swept over him.

During the night there was a great roaring in his dreams and he felt that he had been caught in a rockslide and that his head had been hurt. A sudden blaze of light against his closed eyelids jerked him awake and he lay there in the dark, filled with unreasoning fear, as the great sound rumbled and died. Only then did he realize that it was raining heavily; the roar of drops on the grass thatch of the roof was what had penetrated his dreams. Then the lightning blazed again and, for a long instant, illuminated the interior of the house with a strange blue light that clearly showed him the fire stones, the pots, the dark and silent form of his mother sleeping soundly on her petlatl, the billowing of the mat in front of the doorway and the runnel of water that ran in onto the earthen floor. Then the light was gone and the thunder rolled again with a great noise that must have filled the entire valley. The gods at play, the priests said, tearing apart mountains and throwing giant boulders about as they had once thrown them to seal the exit here.

Chimal's head hurt when he sat up; that part of the dream had been true enough. He had drunk too much of the octli. His mother had been worried, he remembered that now, since drunkenness was a sacred thing and should only be indulged in during certain festivals. Well, he had made his own festival. He pushed aside the mat and stepped out into the rain, let it wash over his upturned face and run down the length of his naked body. It trickled into his open mouth and he swallowed its sweet substance. His head felt better and his skin was washed clean. There would be water now for the corn and the crop might be a good one after all.

Lightning streaked across the sky and he thought at once of the spear of light he had seen after the sun had set. Had it been the same sort of thing? No, this lightning writhed and twisted like a beheaded snake while the other light had been straight as an arrow.

The rain no longer felt good; it was chilling him, and he did not want to think about what he had seen the evening before. He turned and went quickly back inside.

In the morning the drums drew him slowly awake as they had every day of his life. His mother was already up and blowing the embers of the banked fire into life. She said nothing, but he could feel the disapproval in the angle of her back as she turned away from him. When he touched his face he found that his jaw was bristly with stubble: this would be a good time to take care of it. He filled a bowl with water and crumbled into it some copal-xocotl, the dried root of the soap tree. Then, taking the bowl and his knife, he went out behind the house where the first rays of the sun struck him. The clouds were gone and it was going to be a clear day. He lathered his face well and found a pool of water on the rock ledge that reflected his

26

image and helped him to shave cleanly.

When he was through his cheeks were smooth and he rubbed them with his fingers and turned his head back and forth to see if he had missed any spots. It was almost a stranger who looked back at him from the water, so much had he changed in the last few years. His jaw was wide and square, very different from his father's everyone said, who had been a small-boned man. Even now, alone, his lips were tight shut as though to lock in any stray words, his mouth as expressionless as a line drawn in the sand. He had many years of experience in not answering. Even his deep gray eyes were secretive below the heavy brow ridge. His blond hair, hanging down straight all around his head and cut off on an even line, was a concealment that covered his high forehead. The boy he used to know was gone and had been replaced by a man he did not know. What did the events of the past days mean, the strange feelings that tore at him and the even stranger things he had seen? Why was he not at peace like all the others?

As he became aware that someone had walked up behind him a face moved into view in the reflection, swimming against the blue sky: Cuauhtemoc, the leader of his clan. Graying and lined, stern and unsmiling.

"I have come to talk about your marriage," the imaged head said.

Chimal hurled the bowl of soapy water into it and the reflection burst into a thousand fragments and vanished.

When he stood and turned about Chimal discovered that he was some inches taller than the leader; they had not met to talk for a very long time. Everything that he could think to say seemed wrong, so he said nothing. Cuauhtemoc squinted into the rising sun and rubbed at his jaw with work-calloused fingers.

"We must keep the clans bound together. That is," he lowered his voice, "Omeyocan's will. There is a girl Malinche who is the right age and you are the right age. You will be married soon after the ripening corn festival. You know the girl?"

"Of course I know her. That is why I do not wish to marry her."

Cuauhtemoc was surprised. Not only did his eyes widen but he touched his finger to his cheek in the gesture which means *I am surprised*. "What you wish does not matter.

You have been taught to obey. There is no other girl suitable, the matchmaker has said so."

"I do not wish to marry this girl, or any other girl. Not now. I do not wish to be married at this time . . ."

"You were very strange when you were a boy and the priests knew about it and they beat you. That was very good for you and I thought you would be all right. Now you talk the same way you did when you were young. If you do not do what I tell you to do then . . ." he groped for the alternatives. "Then I shall have to tell the priests."

The memory of that black knife slipping into the whiteness inside Popoca's head stood suddenly clear before Chimal's eyes. If the priests thought that he was possessed by a god they would release him from the burden as well. So it was like that, he suddenly realized. Only two courses were open to him; there had never been any other choice. He could do as all the others did—or he could die. The choice was his.

"I'll marry the girl," he said and turned to pick up the container of nightsoil to take to the fields.

5

Someone passed a cup of octli and Chimal buried his face in it, breathing in the sour, strong odor, before he drank. He was alone on the newly woven grass mat, yet was surrounded on all sides by noisy members of his and Malinche's clans. They mixed, talked, even shouted to be heard, while the young girls were busy with the jugs of octli. They sat in the sandy area, now swept clean, that was in the center of the village, and it was barely big enough to hold them all. Chimal turned and saw his mother, smiling as he had not seen her smile in years, and he turned away so quickly that the octli slopped over onto his tilmantl, his marriage cloak new and white and specially woven for the occasion. He brushed at the sticky liquid—then stopped as a sudden hush came over the crowd.

"She is coming," someone whispered, and there was a stir of motion as everyone turned to look. Chimal stared into the now almost empty cup, nor did he glance up when the guests moved aside to let the matchmaker by. The old woman staggered under the weight of the bride to be, but she had carried burdens all her life and this was her duty. She stopped at the edge of the mat and carefully let Malinche step onto it. Malinche also wore a new white cloak, and her moonface had been rubbed with peanut oil so that her skin would glisten and be more attractive. With shifting motions she settled into a relaxed kneeling position, very much like a dog making itself comfortable, and turned her round eyes to Cuauhtemoc who rose and spread his arms impressively. As leader of the groom's clan he had the right to speak first. He cleared his throat and spat into the sand.

"Here we are together for an important binding of the clans. You will remember that when Yotihuac died during the hunger of the time when the corn did not ripen, he had a wife and her name is Quiauh and she is here among us, and he had a son and his name is Chimal and he sits here on the mat . . ."

Chimal did not listen. He had been to other weddings and this one would be no different. The leaders of the clans would make long speeches that put everyone to sleep, then the matchmaker would make a long speech and others who felt moved by the occasion would also make long speeches. Many of the guests would doze and much octli would be drunk, and finally, when it was almost sunset, the knot would be tied in their cloaks that would bind them together for life. Even then there would be more speeches. Only when it was close to dark would the ceremony end and the bride would go home with her family. Malinche also had no father, he had died from a bite by a rattlesnake the year before, but she had uncles and brothers. They would take her and many of them would sleep with her that night. Since she was of their clan it was only fair that they save Chimal from the ghostly dangers of marriage by taking whatever curses there were unto themselves. Only on the next night would she move into his house.

He was aware of all these things and he did not care. Though he knew that he was young, at this moment he felt that his days were almost over. He could see the future and the rest of his life as clearly as if he had already lived it, because it would be unchanging and no different from

29

the lives of all the others around him. Malinche would make his tortillas twice a day and bear a child once a year. He would plant the corn and reap the corn and each day would be like every other day and he would then be old, and very soon after that he would be dead.

That was the way it must be. He held his hand out for more octli and his cup was refilled. That was the way it would be. There was nothing else, and he could not think of anything else. When his mind veered away from the proper thoughts that he should be thinking he quickly dragged them back and drank some more from his cup. He would remain silent, and empty his mind of thoughts. A shadow swept across the sand and touched them with a passing moment of darkness as a great vulture landed on the rooftree of a nearby house. It was dusty and tattered and, like an old woman arranging her robe, it moved its wings and waddled back and forth as it settled down. First it looked at him with one cold eye, then with the other. Its eyes were as round as Malinche's and just as empty. Its back was wickedly curved and, like the feathers of its ruff, stained with gore.

It was later and the vulture had long since departed. Everything here was too alive: it wanted its meat safely dead. The long ceremony was finally drawing to its end. The leaders of both clans came forward solemnly and laid hands on the white tilmantli, then prepared to tie the marriage cloaks together. Chimal blinked at the rough hands that fumbled with the corner of the fabric and, in an instant, from nothing to everything, the red madness possessed him. It was the way he had felt that day at the pool only much stronger. There was only one thing that could be done, a single thing that *had* to be done, and no other course was possible to take.

He jumped to his feet and pulled his cloak free of the clasping fingers.

"No, I won't do it," he shouted in a voice roughened by the octli he had drunk. "I will not marry her or anyone else. You cannot force me to."

He strode away in the dusk through a shocked silence and no one thought to reach out and stop him.

6

If the people of the village were watching, they did not reveal themselves. Some of the door covers stirred in the breeze that had sprung up just after dawn, but nothing moved in the darkness behind them.

Chimal walked with his head up, stepping out so strongly that the two priests in their ground-length cloaks had trouble keeping pace with him. His mother had cried out when they had come for him, soon after daybreak, a single shout of pain as though she had seen him die at that moment. They had stood in the doorway, black as two messengers of death, and had asked for him, their weapons ready in case he should resist. Each of them carried a maquahuitl, the deadliest of all the Aztec weapons: the obsidian blades that were set into the hardwood handle were sharp enough to sever a man's head with a single blow. They had not needed this threat of violence, quite the opposite in fact. Chimal had been behind the house when he heard their voices. "To the temple then," he had answered, throwing his cloak over his shoulders and knotting it while he walked. The young priests had to hurry to catch up.

He knew that he should be walking in terror of what might await him at the temple, yet, for some unaccountable reason, he was elated. Not happy, no one could be happy when going to face the priests, but so great was his feeling of rightness that he could ignore the dark shadow of the future. It was as though a great burden had been lifted from his mind and, in truth, it had. For the first time, since he had been a small child, he had not lied to conceal his thoughts: he had spoken out what he knew to be true in defiance of everyone. He did not know where it would end, but at this instant did not really care.

They were waiting for him at the pyramid and there was no question now of his walking on alone. The priests blocked his way and two of the strongest took him by the arms: he made no attempt to free himself as they led him up the steps to the temple on the summit. He had never entered here before; normally only priests passed through the carved doorway with its frieze of serpents disgorging skeletons. When they paused at the entranceway some of his elation seeped out before this ominous prospect. He turned away from it to look out across the valley.

From this height he could see the entire length of the river. From the grove of trees to the south it emerged and meandered between the steep banks, cutting between the two villages, then laid a course of golden sand until it vanished into the swamp near at hand. Beyond the swamp rose the rock barrier and he could see more tall mountains in the distance. . . .

"Bring the one in," Citlallatonac's voice spoke from the temple, and they pushed him inside.

The first priest was sitting cross-legged on an ornamented block of stone before a statue of Coatlicue. In the half light of the temple the goddess was hideously life-like, glazed and painted and decorated with gems and gold plates. Her twin heads looked at him and her claw-handed arms appeared ready to seize.

"You have disobeyed the clan leaders," the first priest said loudly. The other priests stepped back so that Chimal could approach him. Chimal came close, and when he did so he saw that the priest was older than he had thought. His hair, matted with blood and dirt and unwashed for years, had the desired frightening effect, as did the blood on his death-symboled robe. But the priests's eyes were sunk deep into his head and were watery red: his neck was as scrawny and wrinkled as that of a turkey. His skin had a waxy pallor except where patches of red powder had been dusted on his cheeks to simulate good health. Chimal looked at the priest and did not answer.

"You have disobeyed. Do you know the penalty?" The old man's voice cracked with rage.

"I did not disobey, therefore there is no penalty."

The priest half rose with astonishment when he heard these calmly spoken words, then he dropped back and huddled down, his eyes narrowed with anger. "You spoke this way once before and you were beaten, Chimal. You do not argue with a priest."

"I am not arguing, revered Citlallatonac, but merely explaining what has happened . . ."

"I do not like the sound of your explaining," the priest broke in. "Do you not know your place in this world? You were taught it in the temple school along with all the other boys. The gods rule. The priests interpret and interpose. The people obey. Your duty is to obey and nothing else."

"I do my duty. I obey the gods. I do not obey my fellow men when they are at odds with the word of the gods. It would be blasphemy to do that, the penalty for which is death. Since I do not wish to die I obey the gods even though mortal men grow angry at me."

The priest blinked, then picked a bit of matter from the corner of one eye with the tip of his grimy forefinger. "What is the meaning of your words," he finally said, and there was a touch of hesitancy in his voice. "The gods have ordered your wedding."

"That they have not—men have done that. It is written in the holy words that man is to marry and be fruitful and woman is to marry and be fruitful. But it does *not* say what age they should be married at, or that they must be forced to marry against their will."

"Men marry at twenty-one, women at sixteen . . ."

"That is the common custom, but only a custom. It does not have the weight of law . . ."

"You argued before," the priest said shrilly, "and were beaten. You can be beaten again. . . ."

"A boy is beaten. You do not beat a man for speaking the truth. I ask only that the law of the gods be followed—how can you punish me for that?"

"Bring me the books of the law," the first priest shouted to the others waiting outside. "This one must be shown the truth before he is punished. I remember no laws like these."

In a quiet voice Chimal said, "I remember them clearly. They are as I have told you." The old priest sat back, blinking angrily in the shaft of sunlight that fell upon him. The bar of light, the priest's face, stirred Chimal's memory and he spoke the words almost as a dare. "I remember also what you told us about the sun and the stars, you read from the books. The sun is a ball of burning gas, didn't you say that, which is moved by the gods? Or did you say the sun was set in a great shell of diamond?"

"What are you saying about the sun?" the priest asked, frowning.

33

"Nothing," Chimal said. Something, he thought to himself, something that I dare not say aloud or I will soon be as dead as Popoca who first saw the ray. I have seen it too, and it was just like the sun shining on water or on diamond. Why had the priests not told them of the thing in the sky that made that flash of light? He broke off these thoughts as the priests carried in the sacred volumes.

The books were bound with human skin and were ancient and revered: on festival days the priests read parts from them. Now they placed them on the stone ledge and withdrew. Citlallatonac pushed at them, holding first one up to the light, then the other.

"You want to read the second book of Tezcatlipoca," Chimal said. "And what I speak about is on the thirteenth or fourteenth page."

A book dropped with a sharp noise and the priest turned wide eyes upon Chimal. "How do you know that?"

"Because I have been told and I remember. That is what was said aloud, and I remember the page number being spoken."

"You can read, that is how you know this. You have come secretly to the temple to read the forbidden books . . ."

"Don't be silly, old man. I have never been to this temple before. I remember, that is all." Some demon goaded Chimal on in the face of the priest's astonishment. "And I *can* read, if you must know. That is not forbidden either. In the temple school I learned my numbers, as did all the other children, and I learned to write my name, just as they did. When the others were taught the writing of their names I listened and learned as well and therefore know the sounds of all the letters. It was really very simple."

The priest was beyond words and did not answer. Instead he groped through the tumbled books until he found the one Chimal had named, then turned the pages slowly, shaping the words aloud as he read. He read, turned back the page and read again—then dropped the book.

"You see I am correct," Chimal told him. "I shall marry, soon, to one of my own choosing after I have consulted long and well with the matchmaker and the clan leader. That is the way to do it by law . . ."

34

"Do not tell me the law, small man! I am the first priest and I am the law and you will obey me."

"We all obey, great Citlallatonac," Chimal answered quietly. "None of us are above the law and all of us have our duties."

"Do you mean me? Do you dare to mention the duties of a priest, you a . . . nothing? I can kill you."

"Why? I have done nothing wrong."

The priest was on his feet, screeching in anger now, looking up into Chimal's face and spattering him with saliva as the words burst from his lips.

"You argue with me, you pretend to know the law better than I do, you read though you were never taught to read. You are possessed by one of the black gods and I know it, and I shall release that god from inside your head."

Angry himself, but coldly angry, Chimal could not keep a grimace of distaste from his mouth. "Is that all you know, priest? Kill a man who disagrees with you—even though he is right and you are wrong? What kind of a priest does that make of you?"

With a wordless scream the priest raised both his fists and brought them down together to strike Chimal and tear the voice from his mouth. Chimal seized the old man's wrists and held them easily even though the priest struggled to free himself. There was a rush of feet as the horrified onlookers ran to help the first priest. As soon as they touched him, Chimal released his hands and stepped back, smiling crookedly.

Then it happened. The old man raised his arms again, opened his mouth wide until his almost gumless jaws were pinkly visible—then cried out, but no words came forth.

There was a screech, more of pain than anger now, and the priest crashed to the floor like a felled tree. His head struck the stone with a hollow thudding sound and he lay motionless, his eyes partly open and the yellowed whites showing, while a bubble of froth foamed on his lips.

The other priests rushed to his side, picked him up and carried him away, and Chimal was struck down from behind by one of them who carried a club. If it had been another weapon it would have killed him, and even though Chimal was unconscious this did not stop the

priests from kicking his inert body before they carried him
away too.

As the sun cleared the mountains it shone through the
openings in the wall and struck fire from the jewels in
Coatlicue's serpent's eyes. The books of the law lay,
neglected, where they had been dropped.

7

"It looks like old Citlallatonac is very sick," the priest said
in a low voice while he checked the barred entrance to
Chimal's cell. It was sealed by heavy bars of wood, each
thicker than a man's leg, that were seated into holes in the
stone of the doorframe. They were kept in place by a
heavier, notched log that was pegged to the wall beyond
the prisoner's reach: it could only be opened from the outside. Not that Chimal was free to even attempt this, since
his wrists and ankles were tied together with unbreakable
maguey fibre.

"You made him sick," the young priest added, rattling
the heavy bars. He and Chimal were of the same age and
had been in the temple school together. "I don't know why
you did it. You were in trouble in school, but I guess we
all were, more or less, that is the way boys are. I never
thought that you would end up doing this." Almost as a
conversational punctuation mark he jabbed his spear between the bars and into Chimal's side. Chimal rolled away
as the obsidian point dug into the muscle of his side and
blood ran from the wound.

The priest left and Chimal was alone again. There was
a narrow slit in the stone wall, high up, that let in a dusty
beam of sunlight. Voices penetrated too, excited shouts
and an occasional wail of fear from some woman.

They came, one after another, everyone, as word spread
through the villages. From Zaachila they ran through the
fields, tumbling like ants from a disturbed nest, to the
riverbed and across the sand. On the other side they met
the people from Quilapa, running, all of them, in fear.

They grouped around the base of the pyramid in a solid mass, shouting and calling to one another for any bits of news that might be known. The noise died only when a priest appeared from the temple above and walked slowly down the steps, his hands raised for silence. He stopped when he reached the sacrificial stone. His name was Itzcoatl and he was in charge of the temple school. He was a stern, tall man in his middle years, with matted blond hair that fell below his shoulders. Most people thought that some day he would be first priest.

"Citlallatonac is ill," he called out, and a low moan was breathed by the listening crowd. "He is resting now and we attend him. He breathes but he is not awake."

"What is the illness that struck him down so quickly?" one of the clan leaders called out from below.

Itzcoatl was slow in answering; his black-rimmed fingernail picked at a dried spot of blood on his robe. "It was a man who fought with him," he finally said. Silence stifled the crowd. "We have the man locked away so we may question him later, then kill him. He is mad or he is possessed by a demon. We will find out. He did not strike Citlallatonac but it is possible that he put a curse on him. The name of this man is Chimal."

The people stirred and hummed like disturbed bees at this news, and drew apart. They were still closely packed, even more so now as they moved away from Quiauh, as though her touch might be poisonous. Chimal's mother stood in the center of the open space with her head lowered and her hands clasped before her, a small and lonely figure.

This was the way the day went. The sun mounted higher and the people remained, waiting. Quiauh stayed as well, but she moved off to one side of the crowd where she would be alone: no one spoke to her or even looked her way. Some people sat on the ground or talked in low voices, others went into the fields to relieve themselves but they always returned. The villages were deserted and, one by one, the cooking fires went out. When the wind was right the dogs, who had not been watered or fed, could be heard barking, but no one paid attention to them.

By evening it was reported that the first priest had regained consciousness, but was still troubled. He could move neither his right hand nor his right leg and he had trouble speaking. The tension in the crowd grew perceptibly as the sun reddened and sank behind the hills. Once it had dropped from sight the people of Zaachila hurried, reluctantly, back to their village. They had to be across the river by dark—for this was the time when Coatlicue walked. They would not know what was happening at the temple, but at least they would be sleeping on their own mats this night. For the villagers of Quilapa a long night stretched ahead. They brought bundles of straw and cornstalks and made torches. Though the babies were nursed no one else ate, nor, in their terror, were they hungry.

The crackling torches held back the darkness of the night and some people laid their heads on their knees and dozed, but very few. Most just sat and watched the temple and waited. The praying voices of the priests came dimly down to them and the constant beating of the drums shook the air like the heartbeat of the temple.

Citlallatonac did not get better that night, but he did not get worse either. He would live and say the morning prayers, and then, during the coming day, the priests would meet in solemn assembly and a new first priest would be elected and the rituals performed that established him in that office. Everything would be all right. Everything *had* to be all right.

There was a stirring among the watchers when the morning star rose. This was the planet that heralded the dawn and the signal for the priests to once more beg Huitzilopochtli, the Hummingbird Wizard, to come to their aid. He was the only one who could successfully fight the powers of darkness, and ever since he had brought the Aztec people into being he had watched over them. Each night they called to him with prayers and he went forth with his thunderbolts and fought the night and the stars and defeated them so that they retreated and the sun could rise again.

Huitzilopochtli had always come to the aid of his people, though he had to be induced with sacrifices and the proper prayers. Had not the sun risen every day to prove it? Proper prayers, that was the important thing, proper prayers.

Only the first priest could speak these prayers.

The thought was unspeakable yet it had been there all

the night. The fear was still there like a heavy presence when priests with smoking torches emerged from the temple to light the way for the first priest. He came out slowly, half carried by two of the younger priests. He stumbled with his left leg, but his right leg only dragged limply behind him. They took him to the altar and held him up while the sacrifices were performed. Three turkeys and a dog were sacrificed this time because much help was needed. One by one the hearts were torn out and placed carefully in Citlallatonac's clasping left hand. His fingers clamped down tight until blood ran from between his fingers and dripped to the stone, but his head hung at a strange angle and his mouth drooped open.

It was time for the prayer.

The drums and the chanting stopped and the silence was absolute. Citlallatonac opened his mouth and the cords in his neck stood out tautly as he struggled to speak. Instead of words he emitted only a harsh croaking sound and a long dollop of saliva hung down, longer and longer, from his drooping lip.

He struggled even harder then, writhing against the hands that held him up, trying to force words through his useless throat, until his face flushed with the effort. He tried too hard, because, suddenly, he jerked in pain, as though he were a loose-limbed doll being tossed into the air, then slumped limply.

After this he did not stir again and Itzcoatl ran over and placed his ear to the old man's chest.

"The first priest is dead," he said, and everyone heard these terrible words.

A wail of agony rose up from the assembled mob, and across the river in Zaachila they heard it and knew what it meant. The women clutched their children to them and whimpered, and the men were just as afraid.

At the temple they watched, hoping where there was no hope, looking at the morning star that rose higher in the sky with every passing minute. Soon it was high, higher than they had ever seen it before, because on every other day it had been lost in the light of the rising sun.

Yet on this day there was no glow on the eastern horizon. There was just the all-enveloping darkness.

The sun was not going to rise.

This time the cry that went up from the crowd was not

pain but fear. Fear of the gods and the unending battle of the gods that might swallow up the whole world. Might not the powers of the night now triumph in the darkness so that this night would go on forever? Would the new first priest be able to speak powerful enough prayers to bring back the sun and the daylight that is life?

They screamed and ran. Some of the torches went out and in the darkness panic ruled. People fell and were trampled and no one cared. This could be the end of the world.

Deep under the pyramid Chimal was awakened from uncomfortable sleep by the shouting and the sound of running feet. He could not make out the words. Torchlight flickered and vanished outside the slit. He tried to roll over but found that he could barely move. At least his legs and arms were numb now. He had been bound for what felt like countless hours and at first the agony in his wrists and ankles had been almost unbearable. But then the numbness had come and he could no longer feel if these limbs were even there. All day and all night he had lain there, bound this way, and he was very thirsty. And he had soiled himself, just like a baby; there was nothing else he could do. What was happening outside? He suddenly felt a great weariness and wished that it was all over and that he was safely dead. Small boys do not argue with priests. Neither do men.

There was a movement outside as someone came down the steps, without a light and feeling the wall for guidance. Footsteps up to his cell, and the sound of hands rattling at the bars.

"Who is there?" he cried out, unable to bear the unseen presence in the darkness. His voice was cracked and hoarse. "You've come to kill me at last, haven't you? Why don't you say so?"

There was only the sound of breathing—and the rattle of the locking pin being withdrawn. Then, one by one the heavy bars were drawn from the socket and he knew that someone had entered the cell, was standing near him.

"Who is it?" he shouted, trying to sit up against the wall.

"Chimal," his mother's voice said quietly from the darkness.

At first he did not believe it, and he spoke her name.

40

She knelt by him and he felt her fingers on his face.

"What happened?" he asked her. "What are you doing here—and where are the priests?"

"Citlallatonac is dead. He did not say the prayers and the sun will not rise. The people are mad and howl like dogs and run."

I can believe that, he thought, and for a few moments the same panic touched him, until he remembered that one end is the same as another to a man who is about to die. While he wandered through the seven underworlds it would not matter what happened on the world above.

"You should not have come," he told her, but there was kindness in the words and he felt closer to her than he had for years. "Leave now before the priests find you and use you for a sacrifice as well. Many hearts will be given to Huitzilopochtli if he is to fight a winning battle against the night and stars now when they are so strong."

"I must free you," Quiauh said, feeling for his bindings. "What has happened is my doing, not yours, and you are not the one who should suffer for it."

"It's my fault, true enough. I was fool enough to argue with the old man and he grew excited and then suddenly sick. They are right to blame me."

"No," she said, touching the wrappings on his wrists, then bending over them because she had no knife. "I am to blame because I sinned twenty-two years ago and the punishment should be mine." She began to chew at the tough fibers.

"What do you mean?" Her words made no sense.

Quiauh stopped for a moment and sat up in the darkness and folded her hands in her lap. What must be said had to be said in the right way.

"I am your mother, but your father is not the man you thought. You are the son of Chimal-popoca who was from the village of Zaachila. He came to me and I liked him very much, so I did not refuse him even though I knew it was very wrong. It was night time when he tried to cross back over the river and he was taken by Coatlicue. All of the years since I have waited for her to come and take me as well, but she has not. Hers is a larger vengeance. She wishes to take you in my place."

"I can't believe it," he said, but there was no answer because she was chewing at his bindings again. They parted, strand by strand, until his hands were freed. Quiauh sought the wrappings on his ankles. "Not those, not yet," he gasped as the pain struck his reviving flesh. "Rub my hands. I cannot move them and they hurt."

She took his hands in hers and massaged them softly, yet each touch was like fire.

"Everything in the world seems to be changing," he said, almost sadly. "Perhaps the rules should not be broken. My father died, and you have lived with death ever since. I have seen the flesh that the vultures feed upon and the fire in the sky, and now the night that never ends. Leave me before they find you. There is no place I can escape to."

"You must escape," she said, hearing only the words she wanted as she worked on the bindings of his ankles. To please her, and for the pleasure of feeling his body free again he did not stop her.

"We will go now," she said when he was able to stand on his feet at last. He leaned on her for support as they climbed the stairs, and it was like walking on live coals. There was only silence and darkness beyond the doorway. The stars were clear and sharp and the sun had not risen. Voices murmured above as the priests intoned the rites for the new first priest.

"Good-bye, my son, I shall never see you again."

He nodded, in pain, in the darkness, and could not speak. Her words were true enough: there was no escape from this valley. He held her once, to comfort her, the way she used to hold him when he was small, until she gently pushed him away. "Go now," she said, "and I will return to the village."

Quiauh waited in the doorway until his stumbling figure had vanished into the endless night, then she turned and quietly went back down the stairs to his cell. From the inside she pulled the bars back into place, though she could not seal them there, then seated herself against the far wall. She felt about the stone floor until her fingers touched the bindings she had removed from her son. They were too short to tie now, but she still wrapped them around her wrist and held the ends with her fingers. One piece she placed carefully over her ankles.

Then she sat back, placidly, almost smiling into the darkness.

The waiting was over at last, those years of waiting. She would be at peace soon. They would come and find her here and know that she had released her son. They would kill her but she did not mind.

Death would be far easier to bear.

8

In the darkness someone bumped into Chimal and clutched him; there was an instant of fear as he thought he was captured. But, even as he made a fist to strike out he heard the man, it might even be a woman, moan and release him to run on. Chimal realized that now, during this night, everyone would be just as afraid as he was. He stumbled forward, away from the temple with his hands outstretched before him, until he was separated from the other people. When the pyramid, with the flickering lights on its summit, was just a great shadow in the distance he dropped and put his back against a large boulder and thought very hard.

What shall I do? He almost spoke the words aloud and realized that panic would not help. The darkness was his protection, not his enemy as it was to all the others, and he must make good use of it. What came first. Water, perhaps? No, not now. There was water only in the village and he could not go there. Nor to the river while Coatlicue walked. His thirst would just have to be forgotten: he had been thirsty before.

Could he escape this valley? For many years he had had this thought somewhere in the back of his mind, the priests could not punish you for *thinking* about climbing the cliffs, and at one time or another he had looked at every section of wall of the valley. It could be climbed in some places, but never very far. Either the rock became very smooth or there was an overhang. He had never found a spot that even looked suitable for an attempt.

If he could only fly! Birds left this valley, but he was no bird. Nothing else escaped, other than the water, and he was not water either. But he could swim in water, there might be a way out that way.

Not that he really believed this. His thirst may have had something to do with the decision, and the fact that he was between the temple and the swamp and it would be easy to reach without meeting anyone on the way. There was the need to do something in any case, and this was the easiest way. His feet found a path and he followed it slowly through the darkness, until he could hear the night sounds of the swamp not far ahead. He stopped then, and even retraced his steps because Coatlicue would be in the swamp as well. Then he found a sandy spot off the path and lay down on his back. His side hurt, and so did his head. There were cuts and bruises over most of his body. Above him the stars climbed and he thought it strange to see the summer and fall stars at this early time of the year. Birds called plaintively from the direction of the swamp, wondering where dawn was, and he went to sleep. The familiar spring constellations had returned, so an entire day must have passed without the sun rising.

From time to time he awoke, and the last time he saw the faintest lightening in the east. He put a pebble into his mouth to help him forget the thirst, then sat up and watched the horizon.

A new first priest must have been appointed, probably Itzcoatl, and the prayers were being said. But it was not easy; Huitzilopochtli must be fighting very hard. For a long time the light in the east did not change, then, ever so slowly it brightened until the sun rose above the horizon. It was a red, unhappy sun, but it rose at last. The day had begun and now the search for him would begin as well. Chimal went over the rise to the swamp and splashed into the mud until the water deepened, then pushed aside the floating layer of green with his hands and lowered his face to drink.

It was full daylight now and the sun seemed to be losing its unhealthy reddish cast as it climbed triumphantly up into the sky. Chimal saw his footprints cutting through the mud into the swamp, but it did not matter. There were few places in the valley to hide and the swamp was the only one that could not be quickly searched. They would be after him here. Turning away, he pushed through the waist-high water, heading deeper in.

He had never been this far into the swamp before, nor had anyone else that he knew of, and it was easy to see why. Once the belt of clattering reeds had been crossed at the edge of the water the tall trees began. They stood above the water, on roots like many legs, and their foliage joined overhead. Thick gray growths hung from their branches and trailed in the water, and under the matted leaves and streamers the air was dark and stagnant. And thick with insect life. Mosquitoes and gnats filled his ears with their shrill whining and sought out his skin as he penetrated into the shadow. Within a few minutes his cheeks and arms were puffing up and his skin was splotched with blood where he had smashed the troublesome insects. Finally he dug some of the black and foulsmelling mud from the bottom of the swamp and plastered it onto his exposed skin. This helped a bit, but it kept washing off when he came to the deeper parts and had to swim.

There were greater dangers as well. A green water snake swam toward him, its body wriggling on the surface and its head high and poison fangs ready. He drove it off by splashing at it, then tore off a length of dry branch in case he should encounter more of the deadly reptiles.

Then there was sunlight before him and a narrow strip of water between the trees and the tumbled rock barrier. He climbed out onto a large boulder, grateful for the sun and the relief from the insects.

Swollen black forms, as long as his finger and longer, hung from his body, damp and repellent looking. When he clutched one it burst in his fingers and his hand was suddenly sticky with his own blood. Leeches. He had seen the priests use them. Each one had to be pried off carefully and he did this, until they were all gone and his body was covered with a number of small wounds. After washing off the blood and fragments of leech he looked up at the barrier that rose above him.

He would never be able to climb it. Lips of great boulders, some of them as big as the temple, projected and overhung one another. If one of them could be passed the others waited. Nevertheless it had to be tried, unless a way could be found out at the water level, though this looked equally hopeless. While he considered this he heard a victorious shout and looked up to see a priest standing on the rocks just a few hundred feet away. There were splashes from the swamp and he turned and dived back into the

45

water and the torturous shelter of the trees.

It was a very long day. Chimal was not seen again by his pursuers, but many times he was surrounded by them as they splashed noisily through the swamp. He escaped by holding his breath and hiding under the murky water when they came near, and by staying in the densest, most insect-ridden places that they were hesitant to penetrate. By the late afternoon he was near exhaustion and knew he could not go on very much longer. A scream, and even louder shouting, saved his life—at the expense of one of the searchers. He had been bitten by a water snake, and this accident took the heart out of the other hunters. Chimal heard them moving away from him and he remained, hidden, under an overhanging limb with just his head above the water. His eyelids were so swollen from insect bites that he had to press them apart with his fingers to see clearly.

"Chimal," a voice called in the distance, then again, "Chimal . . . We know you are in there, and you cannot escape. Give yourself to us because we will find you in the end. Come now . . ."

Chimal sank lower in the water and did not bother to answer. He knew as well as they did that there was no final escape. Yet he would still not give himself up to their torture. It would be better to die here in the swamp, die whole and stay in the water. And keep his heart.

As the sky darkened he began to work his way carefully toward the edge of the swamp. He knew that none of them would stay in the water during the night, but they might very well lie hidden among the rocks nearby to see him if he emerged and tried to escape. Pain and exhaustion made thinking difficult, yet he knew he had to have a plan. If he stayed in the deep water he would surely be dead by morning. As soon as it was dark he would go into the reeds close to shore and then decide what to do next. It was hard to think.

He must have been unconscious for some time, there near the water's edge, because when he forced his swollen eyelids open with his fingertips he saw that the stars were out and that all traces of light had vanished from the sky. This troubled him greatly and in his befuddled state he could not be sure why. A breeze stirred the reeds so that they rustled behind him. Then the motion died away and for a moment the air held a hushed evening silence.

At this instant, far off to the left in the direction of the river, he heard an angry hissing.

Coatlicue!

He had forgotten her! Here he was near the river at night, in the water, and he had forgotten her!

He lay there, paralyzed with fear, as a sudden rattle of gravel and running footsteps sounded on the hard ground. His first thought was Coatlicue, then he realized that someone had been hidden close by among the rocks, waiting to take him if he emerged from the swamp. Whoever it was had also heard Coatlicue and had run for his life.

The hissing sounded again, closer.

Since he had escaped in the swamp all day—and since he knew there were men lying in wait for him on shore—he pulled himself slowly back into the water. He did it without thinking: the voice of the goddess had driven all thought from his mind. Slowly, making not a sound, he backed up until the water reached to his waist.

And then Coatlicue appeared over the rise, both heads looking toward him and hissing with loud anger, while the starlight shone on the outstretched claws.

Chimal could not look anymore at his own death; it was too hideous. He took a deep breath and slipped under the water, swimming to keep himself below the surface. He could not escape this way, but he would not have to watch as she trod through the water toward him, then plunged down her claws like some monstrous fisher and pulled him to her.

His lungs burned and still she had not struck. When he could bear it no longer he slowly raised his head and looked out at the empty shore. Dimly, upriver in the distance, there was the echo of a faint hissing.

For a long time Chimal just stood there, the water streaming from his body, while his befuddled mind attempted to understand what had happened. Coatlicue was gone. She had come for him and he had hidden under the water. When he had done this she could not find him so she had gone away.

One thought cut through the fatigue and lifted him so that he whispered it aloud.

"I have outwitted a god. . . ."

What could it all mean? He went out of the water and

lay on the sand that was still warm from the day and thought about it very hard. He was different, he had always known that, even when he was working hard to conceal the difference. He had seen strange things and the gods had not struck him down—and now he had escaped Coatlicue. Had he outwitted a god? He must have. Was he a god? No, he knew better than that. Then how, how . . .

Then he slept, restlessly, waking and sleeping again. His skin was hot and he dreamt, and at times he did not know if he was dreaming awake or asleep. He could have been taken then, easily, but the human watchers had been frightened away and Coatlicue did not return.

Toward dawn the fever must have broken because he awoke, shivering, and very thirsty. He stumbled to the shore and drank from his cupped hands and rubbed water onto his face. He felt sore and bruised from head to toe, so that the many little aches merged into one all-consuming pain. His head still rang with the effects of the fever and his thoughts were clumsy—but one thought kept repeating over and over like the hammering of a ritual drum. He had escaped Coatlicue. For some reason she had not discovered him in the water. Had it been that? It would be easy enough to find out: she would be returning soon and he could wait for her. Once the idea had been planted it burned in his brain. Why not? He had escaped her once—he would do it again. He would look at her again and escape again, that's what he would do.

Yes, that is what he would do, he mumbled to himself, and stumbled off toward the West, following the edge of the swamp. This is where the goddess had first come from and this is where she might reappear. If she did, he would see her again. When the shoreline turned he realized that he had come to the river where it drained into the swamp, and prudence drove him back into the water. Coatlicue guarded the river. It would be dawn soon and he would be safe, far out here in the water with just his head showing, peering through the reeds.

The sky was red and the last stars were fading when she returned. Shivering with fear he remained where he was, but sank deeper into the water until just his eyes were above the surface. Coatlicue never paused but walked heavily along the riverbank, the snakes in her kirtle hissing in response to her two great serpents' heads.

As she passed he rose slowly from the water and watched her go. She went out of sight along the edge of the swamp and he was alone, with the light of another day striking gold fire from the tops of the high peaks before him.

When it was full daylight he followed her.

There was no danger now, Coatlicue only walked by night and it was not forbidden to enter this part of the valley during the day. Elation filled him—he followed the goddess. He had seen her pass and here, beside the hardened mud, he could see signs of her passing. Perhaps she had come this way often because he found himself following what appeared to be a well trodden path. He would have taken it for an ordinary path, used by the men who came to snare the ducks and other birds here, if he had not seen her go this way. Around the swamp the path led, then toward the solid rock of the cliff wall. It was hard to follow on the hard soil and among the boulders, yet he found traces because he knew what to look for. Coatlicue had come this way.

Here there was a cleft in the rock where some ancient fissure had split the wall. Boulders rose on both sides and it did not seem possible that she had gone any other way unless she flew, which perhaps goddesses could do. If she walked she had gone straight ahead.

Chimal started into the rocky cleft just as a rolling wave of rattlesnakes and scorpions poured out of it.

The sight was so shocking, he had never seen more than one of these poisonous creatures at a time before, that he just stood there as death rustled close. Only his natural feelings of repulsion saved his life. He fell back before the deadly things and clambered up a steep boulder, pulling his feet up as the first of them swirled around the base. Drawing himself up higher he threw one hand over the summit of the rock—and a needle of fire lanced down his arm. He was not the first to arrive and there, on his wrist, the large, waxy-yellow scorpion had plunged its sting deep into his flesh.

With a gesture of loathing he shook it to the rock and crushed it under his sandal. More of the poisonous insects had crawled up the easy slope of the other side of the boulder and he stamped on them and kicked them back, then he bruised his wrist against the sharp edge of stone

49

until it bled before he tried to suck out the venom. The greater pain in his arm drowned out all the other minor ones on his ravaged body.

Had that wave of nauseating death been meant for him? There was no way of telling and he did not want to think about it. The world he knew was changing too fast and all of the old rules seemed to be breaking down. He had looked on Coatlicue and lived, followed her and lived. Perhaps the rattlesnakes and the scorpions were one of her attributes that followed naturally after her, the way dew followed the night. He could not begin to understand it. The poison was making him lightheaded—yet elated at the same time. He felt as though he could do anything and that there was no power on Earth, above or below it, that could stop him.

When the last snake and insect had gone on or vanished among the crevices in the rocks, he slid carefully back to the ground and went on up the path. It twisted between great ragged boulders, immense pieces that had dropped from the fractured cliff, then entered the crevice in the cliff itself. The vertical crack was high, but not very deep. Chimal, following what was obviously a well-trodden path, found himself suddenly facing the wall of solid rock.

There was no way out. The trail led to a dead end. He leaned against the rough stone and fought to get his breath. This is what he should have suspected. Because Coatlicue walked the Earth in solid guise did not mean that she was human or had human limitations. She could turn to gas if she wanted to and fly up and out of here. Or perhaps she could walk into the solid rock which would be like air to her. What did it matter—and what was he doing here? Fatigue threatened to overwhelm him and his entire arm was burning from the insect's poisonous bite. He should find a place to hide for the day, or find some food, do anything but remain here. What madness had led him on this strange chase?

He turned away—then jumped aside as he saw the rattlesnake. The snake was in the shadow against the cliff face. It did not move. When he came close he saw that it lay on its side with its jaws open and its eyes filmed. Chimal reached out carefully with his toe—and kicked at it. It merely flopped limply: it was surely dead. But it seemed to be, in some way, attached to the cliff.

50

Curious now, he reached out a cautious hand and touched its cool body. Perhaps the serpents of Coatlicue could emerge from solid rock just as she could enter it. He tugged on the body, harder and harder until it suddenly tore and came away in his hand. When he bent close, and pressed his cheek to the ground, he could see where the snake's blood had stained the sand, and the crushed end of the back portion of its body. It was squashed flat, no thicker than his fingernail, and seemed to be imbedded in the very rock itself. No, there was a hairline crack on each side, almost invisible in the shadows close to the ground. He put his fingertips against it and traced its long length, a crack as straight as an arrow. The line ended suddenly, but when he looked closely he saw that it went straight up now, a thin vertical fissure in the rock.

With his fingers he traced it up, high over his head, then to the left, to another corner, then back down again. Only when his hand had returned to the snake again did he realize the significance of what he had found. The narrow crack traced a high, four sided figure in the face of the cliff.

It was a door!

Could it be? Yes, that explained everything. How Coatlicue had left and how the snakes and scorpions had been admitted. A door, an exit from the valley . . .

When the total impact of this idea hit him he sat down suddenly on the ground, stunned by it. An exit. A way out. It was a way that only the gods used, he would have to consider that carefully, but he had seen Coatlicue twice and she had not seized him. There just might be a way to follow her from the valley. He had to think about it, think hard, but his head hurt so. More important now was thinking about staying alive, so he might be able later to do something about this earth-shaking discovery. The sun was higher in the sky now and the searchers must already be on their way from the villages. He had to hide—and not in the swamp. Another day there would finish him. Clumsily and painfully, he began to run back down the path toward the village of Zaachila.

There were wastelands near the swamp, rock and sand with occasional stands of cactus, with no place to hide in all their emptiness. Panic drove Chimal on now: he expected to meet the searchers coming from the village at any moment. They would be on their way, he knew that. Climbing a rocky slope he came to the outskirts of the maguey fields and saw, on the far side, the first men approaching. He dropped at once and crawled forward between the rows of broad-leaved plants. They were spaced a man's height apart and the earth between them was soft and well tilled. Perhaps . . .

Lying on his side, Chimal scraped desperately with both hands at the loose soil, on a line between two of the plants. When he had scooped out a shallow, grave-like depression he crawled into it and threw the sand back over his legs and body. He would not be hidden from any close inspection, but the needle-tipped leaves reached over him and offered additional concealment. Then he stopped, rigid, as voices called close by.

They were just two furrows away, a half a dozen men, shouting to each other and to someone still out of sight. Chimal could see their feet below the plants and their heads above.

"Ocotre was swollen like a melon from the water snake poison, I thought his skin would burst when they put him on the fire."

"Chimal will burst when we turn him over to the priests—"

"Have you heard? Itzcoatl promises to torture him for an entire month before sacrificing him . . ."

"Only a month?" one of them asked as their voices faded from sight. My people are very fond of me, Chimal thought to himself, and smiled wryly up at the green leaf above his face. He would suck some of its juice as soon as they were gone.

Running footsteps sounded close by, coming directly toward him.

He lay, holding his breath, as they grew loud and a man shouted, right above the spot where he was hiding.

"I'm coming—I have the ocili."

It seemed impossible for him not to see Chimal lying there, and Chimal arched his fingers, ready to reach out and kill the man before he could cry for help. A sandal thudded close beside his head—then the man was gone, his footsteps dying away. He had been calling to the others and had never looked down.

After this Chimal just lay there, his hands shaking,

trying to force a way through the fog that clouded his thoughts, to make a coherent plan. Was there a way to enter the doorway in the rock? Coatlicue knew how to do it, but he shivered away from the idea of following close behind her or of hiding nearby in the rocks. That would be suicide. He reached up and tore a leaf from the maguey and, with one of its own thorns, he made thin slashes so the juice could run out. He licked at this and some time later he was still no closer to a solution to his problem than he had been when he began. The pain was ebbing from his arm and he was half dozing there in his bed of earth when he heard the hesitant shuffle of footsteps slowly coming near him.

Someone knew that he was here and was searching for him.

Cautiously, his fingers crept out and found a smooth stone that fitted neatly into his palm. He would not be easily taken back alive for that month of torture the priests had promised.

The man came into sight, bent low to take advantage of the concealment offered by the maguey plants and looking back over his shoulder as he went. Chimal wondered for a moment what this could mean—then realized that the man was escaping his duty in the swamp. Days of work in the fields had been lost already, and the man who did not work went hungry. This one was going off unseen to take care of his crops: in the confusion that existed in the swamp he would not be missed—and he was undoubtedly planning to return later in the afternoon.

As he came close Chimal saw that he was one of the lucky few in the valley who owned a corn knife made of iron. He held it loosely in one hand and when Chimal looked at it he had a sudden understanding of what he could use that knife for.

Without stopping to think it out he rose as the man passed him and struck out with the stone. The man turned, surprised, just as the stone struck him full in the side of the head. He fell limply to the ground and did not move again. When Chimal took the long, wide-bladed knife from his fingers he saw that the man was still breathing hoarsely. That was good: there had been enough killing. Bending just as low as the man from Zaachila had done he retraced his steps.

There was no one to be seen: the searchers must be

53

deep into the swamp by now. Chimal wished them luck with the leeches and mosquitoes—though the priests were welcome to these discomforts, and perhaps some water snakes as well. Unseen, he slipped up the path between the rocks and once more found himself facing the apparently solid wall of rock.

Nothing had changed. The sun was higher now and flies buzzed about the dead snake. When he bent close he could see that the crack in the stone was still there.

What was inside—Coatlicue waiting?

That did not bear thinking about. He could die here, or he could die at her hands. Hers might even be a quicker death. This was a possible way out of the valley. He must see if he could use it.

The blade of the corn knife was too thick to be forced into the vertical cracks, but the gap below was wider, perhaps held open by the snake's crushed body. He worked the blade in and pulled up on it. Nothing happened, the rock was still immobile rock. Then he tried pushing it in at different spots and levering harder: the results were the same. Yet Coatlicue was able to lift the rock door—why couldn't he? He pushed deeper and tried again, and this time he felt something move. Harder now, harder, he pried up with all the strength of his legs. There was a loud crack and the knifeblade broke off in his hands. He staggered back, holding the worn wooden handle and looking in disbelief at the shining end of the metal stub.

This had to be the end. He was cursed by destruction and death, he saw that now. Because of him the first priest had died and the sun had not risen, he had caused trouble and pain and now he had even broken one of the irreplaceable tools that the people of the valley depended upon for survival. In an agony of self-contempt he jammed the remaining bit of blade under the door again—and heard excited voices on the path behind him.

Someone had found his spoor and had trailed him here. They were close and they would have him and he would be dead.

In anger and fear now he jabbed the broken stump into the crack, back and forth, hating everything. He felt a resistance to the blade and pushed harder, and something gave way. Then he had to fall back as a great table of

54

rock, as thick as his body, swung silently out and away from the cliff.

Sitting there, all he could do was gape. A curved tunnel stretched out of sight into the rock, carved from the solid stone. What lay beyond the curve was not visible.

Was Coatlicue waiting there for him? He had no time to think about it because the voices were closer now, just entering the crevice. Here was the exit he sought—why did he hesitate?

Still clutching the broken corn knife he fell through, scrambling on all fours. As he did this the rock door swung shut behind him as silently as it had opened. The sunlight diminished to a wedge, a crack, a hairline of light—then vanished.

Chimal turned, his heart beating louder than a sacrificial drum in his chest, to face the blackness there.

He took a single, hesitating step forward.

1

Cuix oc ceppa ye tonnemiquiuh?
In yuh quimati moyol, hui!
zan cen tinemico. Ohuaya ohuaya.

Shall we live again, perhaps one more time?
In your heart—you know!
We live but once.

No, he could not start forward, not as easily as that. He fell back against the solid rock of the entrance and pushed his shoulders tight to its surface.

This was where gods walked and he did not belong here. It was asking too much. Certain death waited behind him, on the other side of the stone, but it was the kind of death he knew about; almost an old friend. He had actually gone so far as to press the broken knife under the doorway again before he took a firm grip on his cowardly nature.

"Be afraid, Chimal," he whispered into the darkness. "But do not crawl like an animal." Still shaking he rose and faced the black emptiness ahead. If it was to be death, then death. He would walk forward and face it: he had cowered enough of late.

With the fingertips of his left hand he traced the rough surface of the rock wall, the broken knife was extended before him in bold, though weak, defense. He walked forward, on his toes, keeping his breathing shallow and trying to make no sound at all. The tunnel curved and he was aware of a dim glow ahead. Daylight? The way out of the valley? He went on, but stopped when he saw the source of light.

It was very hard to describe. The tunnel continued on ahead, and seemed to straighten out, but at this spot there was what appeared to be another tunnel opening off to the right. Before this dark opening, set into the rock ceiling above, was something that glowed. There was no other way to talk about it. It was a round area and looked smooth and white, yet light came from it. As though there were a tunnel behind it down which the sun shone, or perhaps a burning torch that shone through this new substance. He could not tell. Slowly he came toward it and looked up at it, but being close did not help him at all to understand what it was. It did not matter now. It gave him light here in the rock, that was enough to know. It was more important to find out where this other tunnel might lead.

Chimal stepped forward to look into the tunnel and stared up at the twin heads of Coatlicue no more than an arm's-length distance from his face.

Inside his chest his heart gave a tremendous leap. Filling his chest as though it would burst, choking his throat and stopping his breathing. She stood there, twice his height, looming over him, fixing him with the steady serpent's gaze of her round red eyes. Her poison fangs were as long as his hand. Her kirtle of living snakes was just below his face. Wreaths of dried human hands and hearts hung about her neck. The great edges of her claws were stained dark with human blood.

She did not move.

Seconds passed before Chimal realized this. Her eyes were open, she looked at him, yet she did not move. Was she sleeping? He had no thought that he could escape her, but he could not bear to be this close to her. The overwhelming fear of her presence started him down the tunnel, and once he began to run he could not stop.

An interminable time later weariness slowed his legs and he tripped and sprawled his length on the rough stone of the tunnel floor. Once down he could not move; he just lay there drawing breath after shuddering breath into the burning cavity of his chest. Still Coatlicue did not strike. When he was able to, he lifted his head and looked back down the tunnel, where the spots of light marked its length, growing dimmer and dimmer until they finally vanished. He was not being followed. The tunnel was still and nothing moved.

"Why?" Chimal asked aloud, but there was no answer

from the solid rock around him. In the silence and the loneliness another kind of fear began to possess him. Would this tunnel ever have an end that emerged outside the valley? Or had he penetrated to some realm of the gods where, like a termite in a tree, he might bore on forever, unnoticed and ignored, in an endless sealed passageway. Everything was so different here that the rules of the valley did not seem to apply, and there was a fogginess in his head when he thought about it. If it were not for the pain and hunger and thirst now, he could almost believe that he had died when the rock had swung shut behind him.

If he were not dead already he would certainly die here in this barren tunnel—or freeze. The rock on which he lay was cold against his skin and he began to shiver once the heat of his exertion had ebbed away. Pulling himself up against the wall he walked on.

After he had passed eight more of the glowing spots of light the tunnel ended. When Chimal came closer he saw that it was not a real ending, but rather that his tunnel came into another tunnel that extended off to the right and left. This new tunnel had smoother walls and was much brighter than his, and the floor was covered with some sort of white substance. He bent to touch it—then jerked his hand away. It was warm—and soft—and for a moment he thought it was some great white animal that stretched out there, a worm of some kind. But, although it was warm and soft, it did not appear to be alive, and he gingerly stepped out onto it.

To his right the tunnel vanished into the distance, its walls unbroken or marked, but to the left he saw dark patches on both walls. This was something different so he turned and went in that direction. When he was close to the first one he saw that it was a door, with a small knob on it, and appeared to be made completely of metal. This would have been a marvel in the valley. He pushed and pulled at the knob but nothing happened. Perhaps it was not a door at all, but served some other more mysterious function. Anything was possible here. He went on, past two more of the plates, and was just coming to the third when it swung open toward him.

He crouched, tense, his fists clenched, the knife-stub ready, waiting to see what emerged.

A black figure stepped through, swung the door shut behind it with a loud clang, and turned to face him. It had the face of a young girl.

Time stopped as each of them stood, unable to move, looking at the other, sharing the same expression of shocked disbelief.

Her face was human and, when he examined her black coverings more closely, her body seemed to be human under their guise. But their strangeness baffled him. A hood of shining black material completely covered her head except for her face, which was thin, very pale and bloodless with dark, widened eyes and thin black eyebrows that met over her nose. She was more than a head shorter than him and had to lean back to look up into his face. The rest of her body was draped tightly in some soft woven material, not unlike that of a priest's gown, that changed to shiny, hard-looking coverings that reached from her knees to the ground. And all about her body were gleaming lengths of metal; fastened to the outside of her arms and legs, girding her body, supporting her head, bending at her joints. Around her waist was a shining belt from which hung unknown dark objects.

When her eyes swept over his bare body, noting the cuts, bruises and clotted blood, she shuddered and her hand flew to her lips. Her fingers were also encased in black.

It was Chimal who spoke first. He was drained of fear, there had been too much of it, and her fright at his presence was obvious.

"Can you talk?" he said. "Who are you?"

She opened her mouth and only gasped, then tried again. She said, "You are not here. It is not possible." Her voice was shrill and weak.

He laughed aloud. "I am here, you see me. Now answer my questions." Emboldened by her fear he reached out and pulled at one of the objects at her waist. It was metal and fastened to her somehow because it did not come free. She squawked and tried to pull away. He let go suddenly and she fell back against the wall.

"Tell me," he said. "Where am I?"

Her frightened eyes still upon him, she touched a square thing at her waist and it dropped into her hand. He thought it might be a weapon and he made ready to take it from her, but she raised it to her face and put her lips near it. Then she spoke.

"Over seventeen porfer staynet Watchman Steel. There is an oboldonol lonen in tunnel one nine nine bay emma, can you read me . . ."

"What are you saying?" he broke in. "You can speak yet some of the words you speak do not mean anything." Her actions baffled him.

She kept talking, still looking at him wide-eyed. When she had finished speaking her incomprehensible mixture of words and nonsense sounds she put the object back at her waist then slid very slowly to a sitting position on the floor of the tunnel. She put her face into her hands and began to sob uncontrollably and ignored him even when he pushed her with his foot.

"What are you doing this for? Why won't you speak words to me that I can understand?"

Her bent head shook with the force of her crying and she took her hands from her face and clutched at something that hung about her neck, on a string that seemed to be made of small metal beads. Chimal pried it from her fingers, angry at her now for her incomprehensible actions and lack of intelligible response, and easily overcame her her feeble attempts to hold onto it. It was black, like everything else about her, and just as baffling. Smaller than his hand, and in shape not unlike a small brick of adobe. There were six deep openings cut into one side and when he turned it toward the light above he saw that each of them had a number at the bottom of the opening.

1   8   6   1   7   3

This was meaningless, as was the shining rod that came out of one end. It did not push or twist, or apparently move in any way. He tried to press on it but it hurt his finger: it was tipped with many small barbs that bit into his skin. Meaningless. He dropped it and the girl snatched it up at once and pressed it to her breast.

Everything about the girl was a mystery. He bent and touched the wide metal band that came up behind her head. It was fixed to the material that covered her entire head, and hinged at the back of her neck so it moved when she did. A shout sounded from far down the tunnel.

Chimal jumped back, his broken-bladed knife ready, as another girl hurried up. She was garbed like the first and paid him not the slightest attention. Bending over the first girl she made comforting noises and spoke to her softly. There were more shouts and a third, almost identical, figure came out of a metal door and joined the first. This one was a man, yet he acted no differently.

Three more of them appeared and Chimal backed away from their growing numbers, even though they continued to ignore him. They helped the first girl to her feet and talked together, all at once, in the same maddening mixture of words and nonsense that the girl had used. They appeared to have reached some kind of decision because, most reluctantly, they admitted Chimal's existence, darting looks at him then turning quickly away. An older man, who had cracked lips and lines about his eyes, even took a pace toward Chimal and looked directly at him, then spoke.

"We go to the morasoraver."

"Where?"

The man, strangely reluctant, and turning away while he said it, repeated the new word over and over again until Chimal could repeat it—although he still did not know its meaning.

"We go to the Master Observer," the man said again, and turned away as though starting down the tunnel. "You come with us."

"Why should I?" Chimal said belligerently. He was tired, hungry and thirsty, and annoyed at these things that he did not understand. "Who are you? What is this place? Answer me." The man just shook his head hopelessly and made little beckoning gestures.

The first girl, her eyes red and her face stained with tears, stepped forward. "Come with us to the Master Observer," she said.

"Answer my questions."

She looked around at the others before answering. "He will answer your questions."

"The Master Observer is a man? Why didn't you tell me that in the beginning?" They did not answer; it was hopeless. He might as well go with them, nothing could be gained by staying here. They must eat and drink and perhaps he would find some of that along the way as well.

"I'll come," he said, starting forward.

They moved quickly away in front of him, leading the way. None of them thought to go behind him. The tunnel came to a branching, then to another, passing many doorways, and soon he was completely confused as to direction. They went down wide stairways, very much like the steps of the pyramid, that led to more caverns below. Some of them were large and contained devices of metal that were incomprehensible. None of them appeared to contain food or water so he did not stop. He was very tired. It seemed a long time before they entered an even higher cavern and faced a man, an older man, who was dressed just like the others except that his coverings were colored a deep red. He must be a leader or a chief, Chimal thought, or even a priest.

"If you are the Master Observer I want you to answer my questions . . ."

The man looked past Chimal, through him, as though he didn't exist, and spoke to the others.

"Where did you find him?"

The girl gave one of those incomprehensible answers that Chimal was beginning to expect by this time. Impatiently, he looked about the chamber at the twisted and brooding, infinitely strange objects. There was a small table against one wall with some unidentifiable things on it, one of which might very well have been a cup. Chimal went to look and saw that one of the containers held a transparent liquid that could be water. He suspected everything in this world now, so he dipped his fingertip into it and tasted it carefully. Water, nothing else. Raising the container to his mouth he drained over half of it at once. It was flat and tasteless, like rain water, but it slaked his thirst well. When he poked at some gray wafers they crumbled to his touch. Chimal picked one up and held it out to the man who was standing close by.

"Is this food?" he asked. The man turned his head away and tried to edge back into the crowd: Chimal took him by the arm and spun him about. "Well, is it? Tell me." Frightened the man nodded a reluctant agreement, then moved swiftly away as soon as he was released. Chimal poked the broken knife into the waistband of his maxtli and began to eat. It was poor stuff, with no more flavor than ashes, but it filled the stomach.

When he had taken the edge from his hunger, Chimal's

attention was drawn back to the affairs in progress. The girl had finished talking and the red-garbed Master Observer was considering her report. He paced before them, hands clasped behind his back and lips pursed with thought: the room was silent while they waited patiently for a decision. The worried lines about his eyes and the wrinkles into which his frowning mouth was permanently set showed that responsibility and decision-making were his accepted duties. Chimal, washing down the food with the remaining water, did not try to interfere again. All of their actions had an air of madness about them, or one of the games children play where they make believe someone isn't there.

"My decision is this," the Master Observer said, turning to face them, his motions heavy with the weight of responsibility. "You have heard the report of Watchman Steel. You know where—" his glance flicked toward Chimal for the first time, then quickly away, "—he was found. Therefore it is my statement that he is from the valley." Some of the audience turned to look at Chimal now, as though this placing had given him a physical existence he had not had before. Tired and sated, Chimal leaned against the wall and pried some of the food from behind his teeth with his tongue and swallowed it.

"Now follow closely my thoughts because they are of the loungst importance. This man is of the valley yet he can not return to the valley. I will tell you why. It is written in the klefg vcbret that the people of the valley, the derrers, shall not know of the Watchers. That is ordained. This one will not then go back to the valley.

"Now listen closely again. He is here, but he is not a Watcher. Only Watchers are permitted here. Can anyone tell me what this means?"

There was a long silence, broken finally by a weak voice which said, "He cannot be here and he cannot be in the valley too."

"Correct," the Master Observer said, with a stately nod. "Then tell us, please, where can he be?"

"That is the question you must ask yourselves, and search your hearts for the answer. A man who cannot be in the valley or cannot be here, then cannot be. That is the truth of it. A man cannot be therefore is not, and a man who is not is therefore dead."

This last word was clear enough, and Chimal had the

63

knife in his hand and his back to the wall in an instant. The others were much slower in understanding, and long seconds passed before someone said, "But he is not dead, he is alive."

The Master Observer nodded and called the speaker from the crowd, a bent man with an old and lined face. "You have spoken correctly, Watchman Strong, and since you see so clearly you will solve the problem for us and arrange that he will be dead." Then he issued completely incomprenhensible instructions to the man, turning back to the others as the watchman left.

"Our tikw is to guard and protect life, that is why we are watchmen. But in his wisdom the Great Designer . . ." when he said this he touched the fingers of his right hand to the small box that hung about his neck and there was a quick flurry of motion as the others did the same, ". . . did provide for all wbwmrieio and there is close by that which we need."

As he finished speaking the elderly watchman returned with a piece of metal the size and shape of a large log of firewood. It fell heavily to the floor when he put it down, and the watchers stepped aside to make room for it. Chimal could see that it had a handle of some kind on one end, with large letters beneath it. He tilted his head to see if he could read them. T . . . U . . . R . . . N . . . Turn. They were the same kind of letters he knew from the temple school.

"Turn," the watchman said, reading aloud.

"Do that, Watchman Strong," the Master Observer ordered.

The man obeyed, twisting on the handle until a loud hissing began. As soon as the noise stopped the end came off in his hand and Chima could see that the object was not solid, but was a metal tube. The watchman reached in and pulled out something shaped like a long stick with bumps and projections on it. A piece of paper fell to the floor as he did this and he looked at it, then handed it to the Master Observer.

"PUIKLING STRUSIIN," he read aloud. "This is for killing. The part with the letter A on it is held in the left hand." He, and everyone else, looked at Watchman Strong as he turned the device over and over in his hands.

"There are many letters in metal," he said. "Here is a C, here a G . . ."

64

"That is understood," the Master Observer snapped. "You will find the part with an A and you will hold it in your left hand."

Trembling under the cold lash of the words, the watchman turned the object around until he found the correct letter and, clutching it in his left hand, held the device for killing triumphantly out before him.

"Next, then. The narrowing of the rear with the letter B on it is held in the right hand," he glanced up as this was quickly accomplished, "then the rear of the device with the letter C is placed against the right shoulder."

They all looked on expectantly as the man raised the thing and poked it against his shoulder, his left hand holding it from underneath and his right hand from the top. The Master Observer observed this, then gave a brief nod of satisfaction.

"Now I read how to kill. The device is pointed at the thing that is to be killed." The Master Observer looked up and realized that he was directly in front of the device. "Not at me, you fool," he spat angrily, and bodily pulled the watchman around until he was facing the side of the room where Chimal stood. The others moved back to each side and waited expectantly. The Master Observer read on.

"In order to kill, the small lever of metal with the letter D on it, which is on the bottom of the device, must be pulled back with the index finger of the right hand." He looked up at the watchman who was trying vainly to reach the little lever.

"I cannot do it," he said. "My finger is on top and the lever is on the bottom."

"Then turn your bowbed hand over!" the Master Observer shouted, out of patience.

All of this Chimal had been observing with strong feelings of disbelief. Could it be that these people had no experience with weapons or killing? This must be true or why else should they act in this impossible manner. And were they going to kill him—just like this? Only the unrealness of the dreamlike scene had prevented him from acting before. And, in truth, he wanted to see how this strange weapon operated. He had almost waited until it was too late, he realized, as the elderly watchman turned his hand over and his groping finger reached out and depressed the metal lever.

Chimal dived to one side as the thing turned to point at him. As he did so there was a quick blast of heat and one of the devices against the wall behind him exploded and began to burn smokily. People were screaming. Chimal hurled himself into the thick of the crowd and the weapon sought him out and fired again. This time there was a screech of pain and one of the women fell over, the side of her head as scorched and blackened as if it had been thrust into a fire.

Now the large chamber was filled with fearful, running people, and Chimal pushed through them, knocking down any who came in his way. The watchman with the weapon was standing still, the device dangling, his eyes widened with shock. Chimal struck him in the chest with his clenched fist and pulled it away from his weak grip. Now, feeling stronger since he held the killing thing, Chimal turned to face any attack.

There was none, just confusion and a welter of shouted orders. He was ignored again, even though he held the device. He walked through the identically garbed crowd until he found the girl he had first met in the tunnel. He could have picked anyone: perhaps he chose her because he had known her the longest in this strange place. Pulling her by the arm he led her to the exit from the chamber.

"Take me away from here," he ordered.

"Where?" she asked, twisting with weak fright in his grip.

Where? To some place where he could rest and eat some more. "Take me to your home." He pushed her out into the corridor and prodded her spine with his new weapon.

2

In this corridor even the walls were of metal, and other substances he did not recognize, with no sign of rock anywhere. Door after identical door opened from the corridor and Chimal, walking behind the girl, almost ran into her when she stopped abruptly.

"This is mine," she said, still half-dazed with fear of the unknown.

"How do you know?" he asked suspiciously, worrying about traps.

"Because of the number." He looked at the black figures on the metal of the door and grunted, then kicked at the door which flew open. He pushed her in ahead of him, then closed and put his back to the door.

"This is a small house," he said.

"It is a room."

The room was no more than a man's height wide and about twice as long. Something that was probably a sleeping mat lay on the ledge, and cabinets were against the wall. There was another door that he pulled open. It led to an even smaller room that contained a seat with a lid and some devices fixed to the wall. There appeared to be no other way out of this room.

"Do you have food?" he asked.

"No, of course not. Not here."

"You must eat?"

"But not in my *room*. At the teykogh with the others, that is the way it is."

Another strange word, his head ached from so many of them. He had to find out where he was and who these people were, but he needed rest first: fatigue was a gray blanket that threatened to fall and smother him. She would call for help if he went to sleep; there was the box that talked to her that had brought aid when he had first found her.

"Take that off," he ordered, pointing to the belt and hanging things about her waist.

"It is not done with others present," she said, horrified.

Chimal was too tired to argue: he struck her across the face. "Take it off."

Sobbing, the red imprint of his fingers clear on her white skin, she did something to the belt and it loosened and fell to the floor. He threw it against the far wall.

"Is there a way out of this little room with the seat," he asked, and when she shook her head *no* he believed her and pushed her into it. Then he closed the door and lay down against it so that it could not be moved without disturbing him, placed his head on his arm, held the killing thing against his chest and fell instantly asleep.

He awoke after some unknown length of time. The light came from above as it had before. He shifted position on the floor and went to sleep again.

The pushing annoyed him, and he mumbled in his sleep but he did not awake. He moved, to stop the irritation, and something about this bothered him and drove him up out of a heavy and engulfing unconsciousness. When he opened his eyes, thick with sleep, he could not imagine where he was: he blinked at the black figure that was running across the room away from him. Watchman Steel was at the door, opening it, before his befogged senses stirred to life. He heaved himself forward, reaching out, and just managed to clutch her ankle as she started through. Once he touched her all resistance stopped completely and she just lay inert, weeping, as he dragged her across the floor then rose and kicked shut the exit. He leaned against it, shaking his head, trying to wake up. His body was sore all over and he was still tired despite the sleep.

"Where is there water?" he said, stirring her with his toe. She only moaned louder, eyes open and filled with tears, fists clenched at her sides. "I'm not going to hurt you, so stop that. I just want some help." Despite what he said he grew angry when she didn't answer and he slapped her again. "Tell me."

Still sobbing deeply the girl rolled over and pointed to the room where she had been imprisoned. He looked in and saw that the little chair had a cover that lifted on a hinge, and beneath it was a large bowl of water. When he bent to scoop some out the girl screeched incoherently. She was sitting up, shaking her finger, horrified.

"No," she finally gasped out. "No. That water is . . . not for drinking. There, on the wall, the nodren, that water you can drink."

Worried by her obvious alarm, Chimal forced her into the room and made her explain its functions. She would not even look at the seat-bowl, but she filled another bowl on the wall with cold water that ran out of a piece of metal when she touched it the right way. After he had drunk his fill he poked at the other devices in the room and she told him what they were. The shower delighted him. He fixed it so that it ran hot and steaming, then tore off his maxtili and stood under the spray. The door was left open so he could watch the girl, and he paid no attention when she screamed again and ran to face the far wall, trembling. Her actions were so inexplicable that he did not attempt to understand, nor care what she did, as long as she did not try to escape again. When he pressed the button that made the soap foam it hurt, but his cuts felt better afterwards. Then he worked the handles to make the water the coldest it could be, before using the other control that blew warm air on him. While his body was drying he rinsed out his maxtili in the bowl-chair that she would not look at, then squeezed it out and put it back on.

For the first time since he had entered the door in the rock he had a moment to stop and think. Up until now events had pushed him and he had reacted. Now, perhaps he could get some answers to the multitude of questions that filled his head.

"Turn around and stop that noise," he told the girl, and seated himself on the sleeping mat. It was very comfortable.

Her fingers were splayed against the wall, as though she were trying to push her way through it, and she remained that way while she turned her head, hesitantly, to look behind her. When she saw him seated she turned to face him and stood stiffly, her hands clasped before her and her fingers turning over and over.

"That's much better." Her face was a white mask, her eyes red rimmed and set in black circles from the continual crying. "Now tell me your name."

"Watchman Steel."

"All right, Steel. What do you do here?"

"I do my work, as it is ordered. I am a trepiol mar . . ."

"Not what you do, you yourself, but all of you, here in these tunnels under the mountains."

She shook her head at the question. "I . . . I don't understand you. We each do our ordered task, and serve the Great Designer as is our honor . . ."

"That means nothing, be quiet." They talked the same way, yet some words were new, and he could not make her understand what he wanted to know. He would start from the beginning then, and build things up slowly. "And stop being frightened, I don't want to hurt you. It was your Master Observer who sent for this thing that kills. Sit down. Here, sit beside me."

"I cannot you . . ." She was too horrified to finish.

"I what."

"You are . . . you have not . . . you are uncovered."

Chimal could understand that. These cave people had a taboo about going about uncovered, just as the women in the valley must wear huipil to cover the bare upper parts of their bodies when they went to the temple. "I wear my maxtili," he said, pointing to his loincloth. "I have no other covering here. If you have something I will do as you ask."

"You are sitting on a blanket," she said.

He found that there were layers to this sleeping mat, and the top one was made of soft and rich cloth. When he wrapped it around him the girl visibly relaxed. She did not sit by him, but instead pressed a latch on the wall and a small, backless chair fell into position: she seated herself upon it.

"To begin," he said. "You hide in the rock here, but you know of my valley and my people." She nodded. "Good, so far. You know of us but we do not know of you. How is that?"

"It is ordained, for we are the Watchers."

"And your name is Watchman Steel. Then *why* do you watch us in secret? What are you doing?"

She shook her head helplessly. "I cannot speak. Such knowledge is forbidden. Kill me, it is better. I cannot speak . . ." Her teeth clamped into her lower lip so hard that a thick drop of blood formed and trickled down her chin.

"That is a secret I will have," he told her quietly. "I want to know what is happening. You are of the outside world beyond my valley. You have the metal tools and all the things that we are cut off from, and you know about us—but you keep hidden. I want to know why . . ."

A deep booming, like the striking of a great song, filled the room and Chimal was on his feet instantly, holding ready the thing that kills. "What is that?" he asked, but Watchman Steel was not listening to him.

As the sound came again she dropped to her knees and bent her head over her clasped hands. She was muttering a prayer, or incantation of some kind, and her words were lost in the greater sound. Three times the gong struck, and on the third stroke she hdl up the little box that hung on the third stroke she held up the little box that hung until one of her fingers was bare. On the fourth stroke she pressed down hard on the rod of metal so that it first

70

slipped into the case, then slowly returned. Then she released the box and began to cover her finger again. Before she could do this, Chimal reached down and took her hand, turning it over. There was a small pattern of indentations in her flesh from the barbs on the metal rod, and even some drops of blood. The whole pad of her finger was covered with a pattern of tiny white scars. Steel pulled her hand away and quickly slipped the cloth over the exposed flesh.

"You people do many strange things," he said, and took the box from her hand. She was pulled close to him when he looked in the little windows again. The numbers were the same as before—or were they? Had not in the last number on the right been a three? It was a four now. Curiously, he pushed on the rod, even though it hurt his fingertip. Steel cried out and clawed for the box. The last number was now five. He released it and she pulled away from him, cradling the object, and ran to the far end of the room.

"Very strange things," he said, looking at the dots of blood on his finger. Before he could speak again there was a light tapping on the door and a voice said, "Watchman Steel!"

Chimal sprang silently to her side and clamped his hand over her mouth. Her eyes closed and she shuddered and went limp. It could be a ruse on her part: he held her just as firmly.

"Watchman Steel?" the voice spoke again, and a second one said, "She is not here, open the door and look."

"But think of privacy! What if she is here and we enter?"

"If she is here why doesn't she answer?"

"She did not report for femio last yerfb, she may be ill."

"The Master Observer ordered us to find her and said we must look in her quarters."

"Did he say look for her *in* her quarters or at her quarters? There is a great difference in the meaning."

"He said in."

"Then we must open the door."

As the door began to move tentatively open Chimal pulled it wide and kicked in the stomach the man who was standing outside. He collapsed at once, falling onto the killing thing which he held. There was a second man who

71

tried to run, but he had no weapon and Chimal caught up with him easily and hit him with his fist on the side of the neck and knocked him down, then pulled him back to the room.

Chimal looked down at the three unconscious bodies and wondered what to do. More searchers would come soon, that was certain, so he could not stay here. But where could he hide in this strange place? He needed a guide—and the girl would be easiest to manage. He picked her up and threw her over his shoulder, then took the killing thing. The corridor was empty when he looked out, so he turned and went off swiftly in the opposite direction from which they had come.

There were more doors here, but he had to go a little distance at least before the search began. He took one turning, then another, every moment tense and waiting to meet someone. He was still alone. Another turning brought him to a short hall, carved from rock again, that ended in a large door. Rather than go back he leaned on the handle and swung it open. He had the weapon ready, but there was no one waiting inside. This was a very large cavern that stretched into the distance. It was broken into many aisles that held bins and countless shelves. A storehouse of some kind. This would do until the girl came to, then he would make her lead him to some safer place—and some food. Perhaps there was even food here, that was not an impossible idea. He ran far into the cavern, to a dark aisle where not much light reached, and dumped her onto the floor. She did not stir so he left her there while he prowled through the place, opening boxes and picking things from the shelves. In one of the bins he found many bundles of black cloth that had been sewn in strange shapes. When he pulled one out he realized that the dangling lengths were like arms and legs and that these were the clothes that the watchers wore. He took up two armloads and went back to the unconscious girl. She still had not moved. He dropped his load and, squatting under the light, tried to find the manner in which the garment was closed. The air here was cooler than in Steel's room and he would not mind wearing something to keep his body warm.

After a good deal of experimentation, and cutting one of the garments to ribbons in his anger, he discovered that a small metal button, set under the wearer's chin, could be

72

made to move down if it was turned first. When it moved the cloth parted behind it, opening straight down between the legs and halfway up the back so that the garment almost split in two. He opened a number of the things this way, but threw them away in disgust when he found he could force his legs barely halfway into them. The garments must be made in different sizes and the ones he had found were all of the smallest. There had to be a way of finding the large ones: the girl would know. Chimal went to her but she still lay with her eyes closed, breathing hoarsely: her skin had a grayish tinge to it and, when he touched it, was cool and slightly damp. He wondered if anything was wrong. Perhaps she had been injured when she fell. Moved by curiosity, he twisted the button under her chin and pulled it down as far as it would go and spread the cloth aside. She was not injured as far as he could see. Her skin was white as paper and her ribs poked against it from beneath like hard knuckles. Her breasts were low mounds, like those of a half-grown girl, and he felt no stirrings of desire at all when he looked at her flaccid nakedness. There was a wide belt of some gray substance about her waist, secured at the front by a piece of cord threaded through the ends. He snapped the cord and pulled the belt off and saw that where it had gone around her body, her skin was red and inflamed. When he passed his finger along the inside of the belt it felt both rough and sharp, as though it were lined with many tiny cactus thorns. It was beyond understanding: he threw it aside and looked at the pads that held the flexible rods to her body. Perhaps she was very weak and the rods helped hold her up. But was everyone here that weak? When he pushed at the piece of metal that supported the back of her head it came away, pulling her hood with it. Her hair had been shaved close to her skull and was now only short, dark stubble. None of this could be understood easily. He closed her garment and put the hood into place as he had found it, then sat back on his heels and wondered about these things. He sat there patiently for some time until she stirred and opened her eyes.

"How do you feel now?" he asked.

She blinked rapidly and looked around before she answered. "I'm all right, I think. I feel very tired."

This time Chimal used patience when he talked to her; if he hit her and she started crying again he would learn

73

nothing. "Do you know what these are?" he asked, pointing to the pile of clothing.

"They are vabin—where did you get them?"

"Right here, there are many of them. I wanted one to cover my body but they are all too small."

"They are numbered inside, there, see," she sat up and pointed inside one of the garments.

"I'll show you where they are. You find me the one I can wear."

Steel was ready to help, but she staggered when she tried to rise. He helped her to her feet and in her discomfort she did not seem to be bothered by his touch. When he showed her the bins she checked the numbering and pointed to the last one. "In there, they are the biggest." She closed her eyes and turned her face away when he broke open a bundle and started to pull one of them on. It stretched to a smooth fit and felt warm.

"There, now I look like anyone else," he said, and she glanced at him and relaxed a bit.

"May I go now?" she asked, hesitantly.

"Very soon," he told her, lying. "Just answer a few questions first. Is there any food here?"

"I—don't know. I was only in the warehouse one time before, a long time ago . . ."

"What is that word you used, about this place?"

"Warehouse. A place where things are stored."

"Warehouse. I'll remember the word." And I will learn what a lot of other words mean before I leave this place. "Can you see if there is food here?"

"Yes, I suppose I can look."

Chimal followed a few yards behind her, ready to leap and hold her if she tried to run, but stayed far enough away to give her an illusion of freedom. She did find some tightly sealed bricks that she told him were called emergency rations, things to be eaten when other food was not available. He took them back to the secluded corner he had first found before he opened them.

"It doesn't taste like very much," he told her after he had broken the transparent skin and tasted the paste inside.

"It is very nutritious," she told him, then hesitantly asked for some for herself. He gave a package to her after she had explained what this new word meant.

74

"You have lived here all your life?" he asked, licking his fingers.

"Yes, of course," Steel answered, startled by the question.

Chimal did not respond at once, but frowned in concentration instead. This girl must know all the things he needed to know—but how to get her to tell them? He realized that he had to ask the right questions to get the right answers, as though this were a child's game with different rules. I am a turkey. How can you tell that I am a turkey? What were the proper questions here?

"Do you ever leave here, to go to the world outside the valley?"

She seemed baffled. "Of course not. That is impossible . . ." Her eyes widened suddenly. "I cannot tell you."

Chimal changed the subject quickly. "You know about our gods?" he asked, and she nodded agreement. "Do you know about Coatlicue?" Coatlicue who had entered these tunnels.

"I cannot tell you about that."

"There seems to be very few things that you can tell me about." But he smiled at her when he said it, instead of hitting her as he might have done earlier, and she almost smiled back. He was learning. "Haven't you wondered how I came to the place where you found me?"

"I had not thought about it," Steel admitted frankly: she obviously had little curiosity about things unknown. "How did you get there?"

"I followed Coatlicue in from the valley." Was there no way of getting information out of the girl? What did she want to hear? "I want to return. Do you think I could?"

She sat up and nodded happily. "Yes, that is what you should do."

"Will you help me?"

"Yes . . ." then her face crumpled. "You cannot. You will tell them about us and that is forbidden."

"If I told them—would they believe me? Or would they take me to the temple to release the captive god from my head?"

She thought hard. "Yes, that is what would happen. The priests would kill you at the temple. The others would believe you possessed."

You do know a lot about us, he thought—and I know

nothing at all about you except the fact of your existence. That is going to change. Aloud he said, "I cannot return the way I came, but there must be another way . . ."

"None I know of, except for the vulture feeding." Her hand went to her mouth, covering it, and her eyes widened as she realized she had said too much.

"The vultures, of course," he almost shouted the words. He jumped to his feet and paced back and forth the length of the aisle. "That is what you do, you feed them. You bring them your sacrifices and your dead instead of burning them. That is how the meat got to the ledge, the gods did not bring it."

Steel was horrified. "We do not give them our sacred dead. The vultures eat meat from the tivs." She broke off suddenly. "I cannot tell you anymore. I cannot talk to you because I say things that I should not."

"You'll tell me much more." He reached for her but she shrank back and tears filled her eyes again. This was not the way. "I won't touch you," he said, going to the far end of the aisle, "so you don't have to be frightened." How could he make her help him? His eyes went to the tumbled heap of clothing and to the end of the belt that protruded from beneath. He pulled it out and waved it at her.

"What is this thing?"

"A monasheen, it should not be here."

"Teach me that word. What does it mean?"

"Mortification. It is a holy reminder of purity, to clarify the thoughts in the correct manner." She stopped, gasping, her fingers flying to her waist. A wave of red suffused her face as she realized what had happened. He nodded.

"Yes, it's yours. I took it from you. I have power over you, do you understand that now. Will you take me to the place of the vultures?" When she shook her head no he took a single step toward her and said, "Yes you will. You will take me there so I can return to my people and you will then be able to forget about me. I can do you no harm when I am back in the valley. But if I remain with you, I know what to do with your taboo. I will do more this time than remove your mortification. I will open your clothes, I will take them off—"

She fell, but she did not faint. He did not help her up because he knew that his touch might push her too far and she would then be of no help to him at all. Now it was just fear of what might be done that drove.

"Get up," Chimal said, "and lead me there. There is nothing else that you can do."

He stepped back as she pulled herself up on the shelves. When she started out he went one pace behind her, not touching her, with the killing thing ready in his hand.

"Stay away from people," he warned her. "If anyone tries to stop us I will kill them. So if you call to them *you* will be killing them."

Chimal did not know if his warning meant anything to her, whether she took deserted passages or that this way was normally empty of people, but in any case they encountered no one. Once there was a flicker of motion at a crossways ahead, but when they reached it there was no one there.

It was a very long time before they came to the side cavern that branched off from the main one. Steel, swaying with fatigue, pointed wordlessly to it, but she nodded agreement when Chimal asked her if this was the tunnel that led to their destination. It reminded him very much of the way he had first entered. The flooring was of smooth rock, while the walls and ceilings were rough-hewn, still bearing the marks of the tools that had cut them. There was one important difference here: two thin bars of metal were fastened to the floor and vanished into the distance with the arrow-straight tunnel.

"Leave me," she begged.

"We stay together, every foot of the way." There was no need to tell her yet that he had no intention of leaving the tunnels, that he was just gathering information about them.

It was a very long way and he regretted not taking water with them. Watchman Steel was staggering now and they stopped twice so she could rest. In the end the tunnel emerged into a larger cavern. The metal bars continued across the floor and into another tunnel on the far side.

"What is this?" Chimal asked, looking around at the unknown fittings of the place.

"There is the way," she said, pointing. "You can move that cover to look through, and those are the controls that open the door."

There was a large metal panel set into the wall where she pointed, with a disk in its center. The disk moved aside when he pushed it and he could see out through the opening it revealed. He found himself looking through a cleft between two rocks at the afternoon sky. There, blue in the distance, he could see the cliff and the range of peaks that lay beyond Zaachila. Directly in front of him was a shadowed ledge and the stark silhouette of a vulture. It extended its wings while he watched and launched itself out into the sunlight, soaring away in a great slow circle.

"This is Watchman Steel," he heard her say, and he turned quickly. She was across the cavern and was talking at a metal box that hung on the wall. "The one is here with me. He cannot get away. Come take him at once."

3

Chimal grabbed the girl by the arm, pulling her away from the metal box and throwing her to the floor. The box had a round disk on the front, and buttons, as well as a slotted opening. A voice came from it.

"Watchman Steel, your report has been heard. Now we are checking the ralort. What is your exact location . . ."

Chimal raised the killing thing and pressed the metal lever. It killed black boxes as well. The voice spluttered and stopped and the box exploded with flame.

"That won't help," Steel said, sitting up and rubbing her arm, her lips curved into a cold little smile of success. "They can find out where I called from, so they know you are here. There is no way to escape."

"I can return to the valley. How does that metal door open?"

Reluctantly, she crossed to the spot where a bar with a black handle protruded from the wall, and pulled the bar down. The plate swung outward silently, and daylight flooded the cavern. A vulture, about to land on the ledge outside, frightened by the motion, flapped loudly and soared away. Chimal looked out across the valley, smelling the familiar cool air above the odor of bird excrement.

"They'll kill me at once if I go back there," he said, and pushed the girl out onto the ledge.

"What are you doing?" she gasped, then screamed as he pushed the handle the other way and the door began to close. Her loud wails were cut off suddenly as rock thudded against rock.

There was a rising, whining sound coming from the tunnel behind him, and a gentle breath of air was driving out of its mouth. Chimal ran and put his back against the wall close to the opening and raised the killing thing. The noise increased and the wind from the tunnel blew faster. These people had great powers: what strange thing were they sending after him, to kill him? Chimal pressed his body hard against the rock as the noise grew louder—and from the tunnel burst a platform with many men on it. There was a great squealing and it shuddered and stopped and Chimal saw that the men all carried killing things. He pointed his weapon at them and pulled the lever. Once, twice the flame burst out, striking among the men, then the thing died in his hands and nothing more happened no matter how hard he pulled and, in desperation, he squeezed too hard and the lever broke off. Swinging it like a club he attacked.

Chimal thought he would die before he advanced a foot, and his skin crawled, waiting for the fire to wash over him. But his two blasts had struck among the crowded men and had done fiery work. Some were dead, and others were burned and in pain. Violence and inflicting death were new things to them; but not to Chimal who had lived with these twin inhumanities all of his life. As long as he could move, he would fight. Before a single flame could blast at him he was in among the men, swinging the metal thing about like a flail.

It was an unequal battle. Six men had entered the cavern, yet within the minute two of them were dead and the others wounded and unconscious. Chimal stood over them, panting, waiting for some movement. The last one that had stirred had received a blow on the head and was now as motionless as the others. Throwing away the useless killing thing, he strode over and pushed the handle that opened the feeding door. Watchman Steel was slumped against the rock, as close to the door as she could get, her face buried in her hands. He had to drag her in because she made no move to help herself. She stayed where he dropped her while he removed the wounded and dead from the platform, being careful not to touch the little shining buttons and rods at the front. He was beginning to learn about them. When it had been cleared, curiosity got

79

the better of him and he examined the thing. Underneath there were wheels, such as were sometimes used on children's toys, that rode on the metal bars that were attached to the rock floor. Some power, controlled from the top, must make these wheels turn and move the platform along. The most interesting part was the shield that rose up in the front. It appeared to be as hard as metal, yet it was clear as water: he could look through it as though it were not there.

The platform rode the bars of metal. He followed them with his eye as they crossed the large cavern and vanished into the smaller tunnel ahead. Perhaps he would not have to go back to face any more of the killing things.

"Get up," he ordered the girl, dragging her to her feet when she did not respond at once. "Where does this tunnel go to?" She looked first, in horror, at the wounded men dumped on the floor, then followed his pointing finger. "I don't know," she finally stammered. "Maintenance is not my work. Perhaps it is a maintenance tunnel."

He made her explain what maintenance was before he pushed her to the platform. "What is the name of this?" he asked.

"It is a car."

"Can you make it move? Answer without lying."

Violence and death had drained her of hope. "Yes, yes I can," she answered, almost in a whisper.

"Show me then."

The car was very simple to operate. He put a new killing thing into it and sat beside her while she showed him. One lever made it go forward and back, and the further it was pushed the faster the car went. When it was released it returned to its middle position while a second lever did something that slowed and stopped the car. Chimal started them forward slowly, bending over when they entered the tunnel until he saw that there was a good deal of space between his head and the rock above. The lights, he had learned that word too, moved by faster and faster as he pushed on the lever. Finally, he had it jammed forward as far as it would go and the car raced at a tremendous speed down the tunnel. The walls tore by on each side and the air screamed around the transparent front. Watchman Steel crouched beside him, terrified, and he laughed, then slowed the speed. Ahead of them the row of lights began to curve off to the right and Chimal slowed even more. The curve continued, until they had turned a full right angle, then it straightened out once again. Immediately after this it began to start downward. The slope was gradual, but it continued endlessly. After some minutes of this Chimal stopped the car and ordered Steel out to stand against the wall.

"You're going to leave me here," she wailed.

"Not if you behave, I won't. I just want to see about this tunnel—stand up straight, will you, as straight as you can. Yes, many Chimalman bless me, we're still going down—to where? Nothing lies inside the Earth except the hell where Mixtec, the god of death lives. Are we going there?"

"I . . . I don't know," she said, weakly.

"Or you won't tell me, it is the same thing. Well, if it is to hell, then you are joining me. Get back into the car. I have seen more wonders and strange things these last few days than I have ever dreamed, awake or asleep. Hell can be no stranger than them."

After a period of time the slope flattened out and the tunnel went on, straight and level. Finally, far ahead, light filled the width of the opening and Chimal slowed and approached at a crawling pace. A much larger cavern gradually appeared, well lit and apparently empty. He stopped the car short of it and approached on foot, pushing Watchman Steel before him. They halted at the entrance, peering in.

It was gigantic. A great room as big as the pyramid, carved from the solid rock. The tracks from their tunnel ran across the floor of the chamber and disappeared into another tunnel on the other side. There were lights along the sides and set into the ceiling, but most of the illumination poured in from a great hole in the roof at the far end of the chamber. The light looked like sunlight and the color was very much like the blue of the sky.

"That just cannot be," Chimal said. "We turned away from the valley when we left the place of the vultures, I'll swear to that. Turned away into the living rock and went down—for a long time. That cannot be sunlight—or can it?" A sudden hope swept through him. "If we went down we could have gone through one of the mountains and

81

come out in another valley that is lower than our valley. Your people *do* know a way out of the valley, and this is it."

The light was growing brighter, he realized suddenly, pouring in through the hole above and shining down the long ramp that led up to it. Two tracks, very much like the ones that carried their car, only much larger, ran down the ramp and across the floor, to finally descend through an opening in the floor that was just as large as the one at the far end.

"What is happening?" Chimal asked as the light grew stronger, so brilliant that he could not look in the direction of the opening.

"Come away," Steel said, pulling at his arm. "We must move back."

He did not ask why—he knew why. The light blazed in and then the heat came, blasting and searing his face. They turned and ran, while behind them the light and heat, impossibly, intensified. It was scorching, a living flame playing about them as they threw themselves into the shelter of the car, arms over their eyes. It grew, light as hot as fire splashed about them—and then lessened.

After its passing the air felt chill, and when Chimal opened his eyes they had been so dazzled by the light that at first he could only see darkness and whirling spots of color.

"What was that?" he asked.

"The sun," she said.

When he could finally see again it was nighttime. They went forward once more into the large chamber, now illuminated by the lights above and in the walls. The night sky of stars was visible through the opening, and Chimal and the girl walked slowly up the ramp toward it, until the ramp leveled off at ground level. The stars above came closer and closer, swooping down brighter and brighter until, when they emerged from the tunnel, they found themselves standing among them. Chimal looked down, with a fear that went beyond understanding, as a glowing star, a disk as big as a tortilla, crawled down his leg and across his foot and vanished. With a slow dignity, born of fear and the effort needed to control it, he turned and led the girl slowly back down the ramp into the welcoming shelter of the cavern.

"Do you understand what has happened?" he asked.

"I don't know, I have heard about these things but I have never seen them before. Dealing with these matters is not my work."

"I know. You're a watchman and that is all you know, and you won't tell me about that either."

She shook her head no, her lips clamped shut in a tight line. He sat, pulling her down next to him, with his back to that opening and the inexplicable mystery of the stars.

"I am thirsty," she said. "There is supposed to be emergency rations at these places so far distant. Those must be cupboards, over there."

"We'll look together."

Behind a thick metal door were packages of rations and transparent containers of water. She showed him how to open a container and he drank his fill before handing it to her. The food was just as tasteless, and just as filling, as before. While he ate he was conscious of a great and overwhelming tiredness. In his mind as well as his body, because the thought of the sun passing close to him and the stars crawling at his feet was so inconceivable that it did not bear thinking about. He wanted to ask the girl more questions but now, for the first time, he was afraid to hear the answers.

"I am going to sleep," he told her, "and I want to find you and the car here when I wake up." He thought for a moment and then, ignoring her feeble bleatings and resistance, he took the box, on its chain of metal beads from around her neck, and weighed it in his hand. "What do you call this?" he asked.

"It is my deus. Please give it back to me."

"I don't want the thing, but I do want you here. Give me your hand." He wrapped the chain around her wrist, and then about his own hand with the deus held inside against his palm. The stone looked hard but he did not care: almost as soon as he closed his eyes he was asleep.

When he awoke the girl was asleep next to him, her arm outstretched and bent so that her body would be as far away from his as possible, and sunlight was streaming through the opening at the top of the ramp. Could the sun be coming again? He had a moment of intense fear and shook the girl rudely awake. Once he was fully awake himself he saw there was no immediate danger and, after unwinding the chain from his stiff fingers, went to get food and water for them both.

"We're going out there again," he said when they were finished, and pushed her up the ramp ahead of him.

They stepped out of the opening onto the blue sky. It felt hard under foot and, when Chimal hit it with the back of the killing thing, a patch of blue chipped away revealing the stone underneath. It made no sense—yet it was the sky. He followed it up and away from him with his eyes, up to the zenith and back down to the mountains on the distant horizon. As his gaze reached them he cried out and staggered back, his sense of balance suddenly disrupted.

The mountains, all of them, were facing toward him, tilted up into the sky at a 45 degree angle.

It was as though the entire world had been pushed up from behind, tipped up on its near edge. He did not know what to think: these events were too impossible. Unable to bear the vertigo he staggered back down the ramp to the solid safety of the hewn chamber. Watchman Steel followed after him.

"What does all this mean?" he asked her. "I can't make myself understand what is happening."

"I can't tell you, this time because I don't know. This isn't my work, I'm a watchman and the maintenance people never talked about this. They must know what it means."

Chimal looked down the darkened tunnel into which the sun had vanished, and could not understand. "We must go on," he said. "I must find out what these things mean. Where does the other car tunnel go?" he asked, pointing to the opening on the far side of the large chamber.

"I don't know. I'm not maintenance."

"You're not much of anything," he told her, with unconscious cruelty. "We'll go on."

He brought the car slowly out of the tunnel and stopped it while she loaded food and water aboard. Now that he was beginning to distrust reality he wanted his own supplies with him. Then they crossed the cavern and plunged into the tunnel opposite. It was flat and straight though, for some reason, the row of lights ahead appeared to be going up hill. Yet they never came to the hill: the tunnel remained perfectly flat. Some difference in the texture of the tunnel appeared ahead and Chimal slowed the car until it was barely moving and crept forward, stopping when he came up the ladder rungs that were set into the solid rock of the tunnel wall. They went up the wall and into a pipe-like opening that had been cut through the ceiling.

We're going to find out where this goes," Chimal said, forcing her out of the car. He stood back while Steel started up the ladder ahead of him. It was about a twenty foot climb up the hole, which was just a bit wider than his shoulders, and two lights were set into it to show the way. The uppermost light was just under a metal lid that covered the top of the shaft.

"Push up against it," he said. "It doesn't seem to be sealed."

It was thin metal, hinged at one side and she opened it easily as she climbed up and through. Chimal followed, up and out of the solid rock and onto the blue sky. He looked up, first at the small white clouds that drifted overhead, and then past them at the valley, with the thin cut of the river and the two brown villages, one on each side, which hung directly over his head.

This time he did fall, pressing himself to the solid surface of the sky and grasping at the edge of the hole. He had the sensation that he was falling straight down, plunging from the sky down to broken death in the fields by the river. When he closed his eyes to cut out the fearful vision it was much better. He felt the solid rock beneath him and the weight of his body pressing against it. After getting slowly to his hands and knees he opened his eyes and looked down. Blue paint of some kind over solid rock; it chipped when he picked at it around the edge of the hole. There were even dusty footprints on it where others had walked, and metal tracks passed close by. Wide-spaced tracks like those that had carried the sun. He went over to them, still on his knees, and clutched the solidity of the blue metal bar. It was worn on the top and shiny. Raising his eyes slowly he followed the tracks across the sky, as they grew closer and closer and finally vanished into a black opening high above, up the smooth curve of the sky. He tried not to think about this or to understand it. Not yet. He had to see everything first. Then, slowly, he rolled onto his back, still clutching the rail.

Above him was the valley, visible from end to end just

as he knew it should look. On both sides were mountains, pointing straight up at him, and more mountains beyond the valley ends. There was the barrier of rock and the swamp at the north end, the wandering path of the river between the fields, the brown buildings and the dark splotches of the two temples, the trees in the south and a glint of silver from the pond. The waterfall was barely visible; but there was no sign of a river leading to it. There were a few mountains there and the blue bowl of the sky began directly behind them.

A flicker of motion caught his eye and he turned just as Steel vanished down the shaft in the rock.

His vertigo was forgotten now as he jumped to his feet and ran to the opening. She was climbing down fast, faster than he would have thought, not looking up. As he started down behind her she reached the tunnel below and jumped from the ladder. He went a few more rungs, then let go and dropped the rest of the way, landing heavily on the solid rock below. Fire washed over his head.

Steel had the killing thing ready, waiting for him to emerge so she could destroy him. Now she gaped at the blackened rungs and wall and, before she could correct her aim, he was upon her, tearing the weapon from her hands.

"Too late for that," he said, throwing it into the car and pulling her around, up against the wall. He clutched her chin tightly, swinging her head back and forth. "Too late to kill me because I know the truth now, all about you watchmen and the world and all the lies I have been told. There is no longer any need for me to ask you questions, now I can *tell* you." He laughed, and surprised himself when he heard the shrill edge to the sound. When he released her she rubbed at the marks his hard grip had made on her chin, but he did not notice this.

"Lies," he told her. "My people have been lied to about everything. It is a lie that we are in a valley on a planet called Earth, that goes around the sun—which is a burning ball of gas. We believed it, all this nonsense, floating planets, burning gas in the air. That flash of fire Popoca saw and that I saw, when the sun set, was a reflection from the tracks, that is all. Our valley is the world, there is nothing else. We live inside a giant cave hollowed out of the rock, secretly watched by your people. Who are you—servants or masters? Or both? You serve us, your

86

maintenance people watch our sun for us and see that it always shines as it should. And they must make the rain come as well. And the river—it really ends in the swamp. Then what do you do with the water—pump it back through a pipe and over the falls again?"

"Yes," she said, holding her deus in both hands and lifting her head high. "We do just that. We watch and protect and keep you from harm, by day and night through all the seasons of the year. For we are the watchmen and we ask nothing for ourselves, asking only to serve."

There was no humor in his laugh. "You serve. You serve badly. Why don't you make the river run strong all the time so we can have water, or bring the rain when we need it? We pray for rain and nothing happens. Aren't the gods listening—or aren't you listening?" In sudden realization he stepped back. "Or are there any gods at all? Coatlicue stands quiet in your caverns and you bring the rain when you wish." With sudden sorrow and realization he said, "Even there you have lied to us, everywhere. There are no gods."

"There are none of your gods—but there is one god, *the* God, the Great Designer. He was the one who made all this, who designed and built it, then breathed life into it so that it began. The sun rose from its tunnel for the first time, took fire and rolled on its first voyage across the sky. The water sprang out from the fall and filled the pool and dampened the waiting river bed. He planted the trees and made the animals and then, when He was ready, He peopled the valley with the Aztecs and placed the Watchers to guard over them. He was strong and sure, and we are strong and sure in His image, and we honor Him and fulfill His trust. We are His children and you are His infants and we watch over you as He has ordained."

Chimal was not impressed. The chant of words and the light in her eyes reminded him very much of the priests and their prayers. If the gods were dead, he did not mind seeing them go at all, but he was not adding any new gods that quickly. Nevertheless he nodded agreement because she had the facts that he must know.

"So it is inside out," he said, "and we have been taught only lies. The ball of gas is gone and the Earth is gone and the stars are little spots of light. The universe is rock, rock, solid rock forever and we live in a little cave hollowed from the center of it." He bent a bit, almost

87

flinching away from the weight of that infinity of rock that surrounded them.

"No, not forever," she said, clasping her hands before her swaying. "There will come a day when the end will come, the chosen day when we will all be set free. For look," she held out her deus, "look at the number of the days since creation. See how they mount and revel in their passing for we are doing our duty by the Great Designer who is father to us all."

"186,175 days since the world began," Chimal said, looking at the numbers displayed. "And you have kept track all that time yourself?"

"No, of course not. I am not yet seventy years old. This deus is a revered treasure given to me when I took the oath of Watchman . . ."

"How old are you?" he asked, thinking he had misunderstood. Seventeen?

"Sixty-eight," she said, and there was a touch of malice at the corners of her smile. "We hew to the days of our service and do our duty, and the faithful are rewarded with the years of their lives. We are not short-lived like the lower animals, the turkey, the snake—or you."

There was no answer for this. Watchman Steel appeared to be in her early twenties. Could she possibly be as old as she claimed? This was one more mystery to go with all the others. In the silence, the tiny, distant whine buzzed like an insect against his consciousness.

The sound grew, and the girl recognized it before he did. Pushing away from the wall she began to run back down the tunnel, in the direction from which they had come. Chimal could catch her easily, but as he turned he recognized the sound too and stopped, poised on the balls of his feet, uncertain.

Another car was coming.

He could catch the girl, but he would be caught himself. Get the killing thing—but what would be the point in killing her? The different courses open to him ticked by, one after the other, and he discarded them. The car would have many men in it with killing things. He would have to flee, that was the wisest course to follow. They would stop to get the girl and that would give him time to get ahead of them. Even as he was deciding this he jumped into the car and pushed the lever forward as far as it would go. Something whined shrilly under the floor of the car and it shot forward like a released arrow. Yet, even as the car picked up speed he realized that this wasn't the complete solution. Was there anything else he could do? Even as he thought this he saw a dark spot in the tunnel ahead: he quickly pulled on the other lever and brought the car to a bucking halt next to the ladder.

It was another exit from the tunnel, with the rungs climbing up through the opening—to what? To the sky overhead, undoubtedly, next to the sun track. This was the second of these openings, and the chances were that there should be more. As soon as he thought of this he jammed the speed lever forward again. By the time he reached the next one—if there was one—he would have figured out what he had to do. It meant taking a chance, but everything in this strange new world meant taking a chance. He had to plan.

Food and water, he must take that with him. Using one hand, he opened the front of his clothing part way and stuffed in as many of the food packages as would fit. Then he drank his fill from the open water container and threw it aside. He would carry the full one with him. The only remaining problem was the car. If it remained below the opening they would know he had gone out that way and would follow him. He did not know if he could escape from a number of men at once. Was there any way that the car could drive on by itself? After all, it would keep moving just as long as the lever was pushed forward: even a child could do that. He looked first at the lever, then around the car. There was nothing to fasten onto, or he would have tied it forward. What about pushing it? He tugged at the seat next to him and it moved slightly. Then, still holding the lever forward with one hand, he stood up carefully and turned around, bracing his back against the panel that held the levers. He pushed one foot against the back of the chair, harder and harder, until something cracked and it toppled over. Yes, if he jammed it in hard it looked as though it would fit nicely. Just as he sat down again he saw the next ladder far ahead.

Chimal was out of the car even before it had stopped moving. He dropped the container of water and the killing thing by the ladder and grabbed up the broken-off seat. The other car was not in sight, but he could hear the growing, far off whine. Bracing the bottom of the broken seat against the other seat he jammed the top against the lever. The car leaped forward, brushing against him and knocking him aside—then slowed and halted as the seat slipped out of position. He ran after it as the sound of the other car grew louder behind him.

This time he turned the seat end for end, with the square-edged bottom against the lever. He jammed it down hard and jumped away. Whining angrily the car lurched forward and kept going, faster and faster. Chimal did not stay to watch it. Head down he pelted back to the ladder as the sound of the approaching car grew closer. He grabbed the water and the killing thing to his chest in one arm and sprang for the ladder, almost running up it, moving as fast as he could with a single arm.

His feet were just clear of the tunnel when the other car shot by underneath. He waited, holding his breath, to hear if they were stopping. The sound grew fainter, slowly and steadily, until it had vanished completely. They had not seen him and they were not stopping. By the time they had discovered what had happened he would be far from this spot. They would not know which of the exits he had used, which would make his chances of escaping that much better. Slowly, a rung at a time, he climbed up to the sky above.

As he emerged from the opening he felt the sunlight warm upon him. Warmer than he was used to.

In sudden fear he turned and saw the great, burning sun rushing down upon him.

4

Standing there, halfway out of the hole, he stood fast for a sudden moment of panic. This passed quickly when he realized that the heat was not increasing and that the sun was growing no closer. It moved, of course, but slowly in order to take a half a day to cross the sky. Even though it was hot, it was not uncomfortably so, and he would be out of the way long before it passed. With calculated speed he threw his burden out upon the blue surface of the sky and closed the cover behind him. He kept his head turned from the sun since its light was blinding when he looked anywhere in its general direction. Then, with the water in one hand the weapon in the other, he put his back to the sun and started toward the north end of the valley, beyond which lay the concealed tunnels of the Watchers. His shadow, black and very long, stretched far out in front of him to the point the way.

Now that he was a little more used to it, there was an excitement to all that was happening that was greater than anything he had ever experienced before in his life. He walked, filled with a great elation, over a wide blue plain. It was flat in front of him, and apparently endless, while on both sides it swept up in an easy curve. Above him, where the sky should have been, the world was suspended. Sharp-tipped mountains came down on both sides and cut across in front of him. It was ground, solid rock beneath his feet, he knew that now, so that it no longer bothered him that the world he had grown up in, the only one that he had known up until a few days ago, hung over his head like a monstrous weight. He was a fly, crawling on the ceiling of the sky, looking down on the poor prisoners trapped below. When he had placed enough distance between himself and the sun he stopped to rest, sitting on the blue sky, and opened the container of water. When he raised it to his lips he looked up at the valley above, at the pyramid and temple almost directly over his head. He put the water down and lay flat on his back, his arms under his head and gazed down on his home. When he looked hard he could almost make out the workers in the fields. The cornfields looked rich and green and would be ready for harvest soon. The people went about their work and their lives without realizing that they were in a prison. Why? And their captors, prisoners themselves in their termite tunnels, what was the hidden reason for their secret observation and the girl's strange talk about the Great Designer?

Yes, he could see tiny figures moving from the fields toward Quilapa. He wondered if they could see him up here, and he moved his arms and legs about and hoped that they could. What would they think? Probably that he was some kind of bird. Maybe he should take the metal weapon and scratch his name in the sky, flake away the blue so that the rock could be seen. CHIMAL it would say, the letters hanging there in the sky, unmoving and unchanging. Let the priests try and explain that one!

Laughing, he rose and picked up his burdens. Now, more than ever, he wanted to find out the reason for all this. There had to be a reason. He walked on.

When he passed over the rock barrier that sealed the end of the valley he looked up with interest. It was real enough, though the great boulders looked like tiny pebbles from here. Beyond the barrier there was no continuation of the valley, just gray rock from which rose the peaks of mountains. Artificial, all of them, made to give an illusion of distance, since the farther peaks were smaller than the ones closest to the valley. Chimal walked over them and past them, determined to see what lay beyond, until he realized that he was walking up a slope.

It was only a small angle at first, but the slope quickly steepened until he was leaning forward, then climbing on all fours. The sky ahead stretched in a monstrous curve up and up until it reached the ground, but he was never going to get there. In a sudden panic, afraid that he was trapped in this barren sky forever, he tried to climb higher. But he slipped on the smooth sky and slid backward. He lay, unmoving, until the fear had ebbed away, then tried to reason his way out of this.

It was obvious that he could not go ahead—but he could always retrace his steps if he had to, so he was not really trapped out here. What about moving to the left and right? He turned and looked up the slope of the sky to the west, where it rose up and up to meet the mountains above. Then he remembered how the tunnel under the sun had appeared to curve upward yet had been flat all the way. There must be two kinds of up in the world outside the valley. The real up and the one that just looked like up, yet appeared to be flat when you walked on it. He took the container and the weapon and started for the mountains high above.

This was the up that really wasn't. It was as though he were walking in a giant tube that turned toward him as he advanced. Down was always beneath his feet, and the horizon advanced steadily. The mountains, which had been above him when he started, were halfway down the sky now, hanging like a jagged-edge curtain before him.

They drifted downward steadily with every step he took forward, until they finally lay directly ahead, pointing at him like so many giant daggers.

When he came to the first mountain he saw that it was lying flat on its side against the sky—and that it only came up to his shoulders! He was past surprise, his senses dulled by days of wonder. The peak of the mountain was tipped with something white and hard, apparently the same substance as the sky only of a different color. He climbed onto the tip of the mountain that lay flat on the ground of the sky and pointed at him like a great wedge, and walked along it until the white ended and he came to the solid rock. What did this mean? He saw the valley, now only halfway up the sky ahead of him and tilted on edge. He tried to imagine how this spot would look from the valley, and closed his eyes to remember better. Looking from the base of the cliff beyond Zaachila you could see over the pyramid to the great mountains outside of the valley, and the even more distant, immense and high mountains, that were so tall that they had snow on their peaks all year round. Snow! He opened his eyes and looked at the shining white substance and laughed. Here he was perched on a snowy mountain peak—if they could see him from the valley he must look like some sort of monstrous giant.

Chimal went on, climbing among the strange, lying-down mountains, until he came to the opening in the rock and the familiar metal rungs that vanished out of sight below. It was another entrance to the tunnels.

He sat down next to it and thought very hard. What should he do next? This was undoubtedly an entrance to the burrows of the Watchers, a part he had not been to yet, since it was far across the valley from the doorway he had first used. He had to go down here, that was certain, since there was no place to hide among the barren rocks. Even if there were a place to hide, his food and water would not last forever. This reminder of the food sent a rumble of hunger through him and he took out a package and opened it.

What was he to do after he entered the burrow? He was as alone as no one had ever been before, with every man's hand turned against him. His people in the valley would kill him on sight, or more probably hamstring him so the priests would have the pleasure of giving him a protracted death. And the master Observer had called him a non-person, therefore a dead person, and they had all worked very hard to put him into that condition. But they had not succeeded! Even their weapons and their cars and all the things they knew had not helped them. He had escaped and he was free—and he intended to stay that way. In which case a plan was needed to insure this condition.

First he would hide his food and water out here among the tumbled rocks. Then he would enter the tunnel and, bit by bit, would explore the surrounding caverns to discover what he could of the secrets of the Watchers. It was not much of a plan—but he did not have any other choice.

When he had finished he hid his supplies, and the empty food wrapper, then threw open the lid of the entrance. The tunnel below was rock floored and began just below the opening. He went along it cautiously until it joined a wider tunnel that had two sets of tracks down the center. There were no cars in sight, nor could he hear any approaching. He had no choice but to go down this tunnel. Holding the killing thing ready he turned right, toward the valley's end and set off between the tracks at an easy trot, covering the ground quickly. He did not like this exposed position and he turned into the first opening that appeared. This proved to be the opening to some circular metal stairs that ran down and around and out of sight in the rock below. Chimal started down them, going steadily even though he became dizzy from the constant turning.

As he went lower he heard a humming sound that grew louder while he descended. At the bottom he came out in a damp tunnel that had a trickle of water down the middle, and the hum was now a hammering roar that filled the shaft with sound. Chimal went forward carefully, alert for any motion, until the tunnel ended in a high cavern that held towering metal objects from which the torrent of sound poured. He had no idea what their function might be. Great round sections of them vanished up into the stone above, and from one of these sections came the dribble of water that ran across the floor and into this tunnel. From the security of the entrance he ran his eye down the row of immense things, to the far end where brighter lights shone on a board of smaller shining objects before which a man sat. Chimal drew back into the tunnel. The man's back was to him and he had certainly not seen the intruder yet. Chimal went back down the tunnel and past the metal stairs. He would see where this led before he went back to the chamber of cars.

As he walked the noise behind him lessened and, when it had died away to a distant hum, he was aware of the sound of running water coming from somewhere ahead. Darkness filled the mouth of the tunnel. He stepped through it onto a ledge above the blackness. A row of lights, curving away to his left, reflected from a dark surface. He realized that he was looking at a vast underground lake: the running water sounded far out ahead of him and small waves trembled the reflections on the surface. The cavern that held the water was vast and the echoes of the falling water sounded on all sides. Where was this place? In his mind he ran through the turnings he had made, and tried to estimate how far he had come. He was much lower than when he had started, and had come north, and then east. Looking up he could imagine his route—and there above would be the swamp at the north end of the valley. Of course! This underground lake lay beneath the swamp and drained it. The things back there in the cavern did something to force the water through pipes back to the waterfall. And where did the row of lights go that skirted the edge of the dark lake? He walked forward to find out.

A ledge had been cut from the rock of the cavern wall and the lights were spaced along it. The rock was slippery and damp and he went carefully. One quarter of the way around the water it went, then ended at another tunnel. Chimal realized that he was tired. Should he go on, or return to his hiding place? That would be the wisest thing to do, but the mystery of these caverns drew him forward. Where did this one lead? He started into it. It was damp, mustier than the other tunnels, though it was lit by the same evenly spaced windows of light. No, not as even as the others, a black gap showed ahead like a missing tooth. When he came up to this spot he saw that one of the smooth objects was inset there—but this one's fire was gone and it was dark. The first one he had seen like this. Perhaps this tunnel was rarely used and this had not been noticed yet. At the end of the tunnel was another round stairway of metal up which he climbed. This emerged into a small room that had a door in one wall. When he put his ear to the door he heard nothing from the other side. He opened it a narrow crack and looked through.

This cavern was quiet, empty, and the largest one he had yet encountered. When he entered it the sound of his footsteps made a tiny rustle in its towering vastness. The lighting here was far less than that of the tunnels, but it was more than enough to show him the size of this cavern, and the paintings that adorned the walls. These were lifelike and strange, people and unusual animals and even odder metal objects. They were marching, all of them, a torrent of frozen motion, going toward the far end of the cavern where there was a doorway flanked by golden statues. The people of the paintings were dressed in different and fantastic ways, and were even of different skin colors, but they all went to a common goal. The pressure of these silent marchers drove him that way too, but not before he looked about him.

The other end of the cavern was sealed with immense boulders that, for some reason, looked familiar to him. Why? He had never been in this place before. He walked closer to them and looked up at their piled magnitude. They reminded him very much of the rock barrier that sealed the end of the valley.

Of course! This was the other side of that same barrier. If the gigantic boulders were removed the valley would be open, and he did not doubt for a second that the powers that had been used to carve these tunnels and build a sun could be used to throw aside the rocks in front of him. From outside there had appeared to be no exit from the valley—because the exit was sealed inside the rock. Could the legends be true? That some day the valley would be open and his people would march forth. To where? Chimal spun about and looked at the high opening at the far end of the chamber. What did it lead to?

He passed between the large, golden statues of a man and a woman that flanked the portal, and then continued down the tunnel beyond. It was wide and straight and patterned with gold designs. Many doors opened off it but he did not examine any of them: that would wait. They doubtless contained many things of interest, but they were not the reason for this passageway. That lay ahead. Faster and faster he walked until he was almost running, up to the great double doors of gold that sealed the end. There was only silence behind them. There was a strange tautness in his chest as he pushed them open.

Beyond was a large chamber, almost as big as the other one, but this one was undecorated and dark, with just a few small lights to show him the way. There was a rear wall and sides, but the far wall was missing. The opening faced out on the star-filled night sky.

It was no sky that Chimal had ever seen before. There was no moon in sight and no valley walls to form a close horizon. And the stars, the stars, the overwhelming quantity of them that broke over him like a wave! The familiar constellations, if they were there, were lost in the infinity of the other stars as numberless as grains of sand. And all of the stars were turning, as though mounted on a great wheel. Some faint, tiny; others blazing like torches of many colors, yet they all were hard and clear points of light without the flickering of the stars above his valley.

What could this mean? In uncomprehending awe he walked forward until he collided with something cold and invisible. The sudden spurt of fear dissipated as he touched it with his hand and realized it must be the same kind of transparent substance that covered the front of the cars. Then this entire wall of the room was a great window, opening out on—what? The window curved outward and when he leaned into it he could see that the stars filled the sky to left and right, above and below. He had a sudden vertigo, as though he were falling and pressed his hand to the window, but the unaccustomed cold of it was strangely ominous and he quickly pulled away. Was this another valley facing the real universe of stars? If so, where was the valley?

Chimal stepped back, unsure, frightened by this new immensity, and as he did he heard a faint sound.

Was it a footstep? He started to jump about when the killing thing was suddenly jerked from his hand. He fell back against the cold window and saw the Master Observer and three other men standing before him, all of them pointing the deadly flame weapon at him.

"You have come at last to the end," the Master Observer said.

THE STARS

1

Danthe togui togui
  hin hambi tegue.
Ndahi togui togui
  hin hambi tegue.
Nbui togui . . .
  hin hambi pengui.

*The river flows, flows
  and never stops.
The wind blows, blows
  and never stops.
The life goes . . .
  without regrets.*

Chimal squared his shoulders, ready to die. The words of
a death chant came automatically to his lips and he spoke
the first phrases before he realized what he was doing. He
spat the words from his mouth and sealed his traitor lips
tight. There were no gods to pray to and the universe was
a place of utter strangeness.

"I am ready to kill you, Chimal," the Master Observer
said, his voice dry and toneless.

"You now know my name and you talk directly to me,
yet you still want to kill me. Why?"

"I will ask and you will answer," the old man said,
ignoring his words. "We have listened to the people in the
valley and learned many things about you, but the most
important thing we cannot find out. Your mother cannot
tell us because she is dead . . ."

"Dead! How, why?"

". . . executed in your place when it was discovered that
she had released you. The priests were very angry. Yet she
seemed almost glad it was happening, and there was even
a smile on her lips."

They did watch the valley, and how closely. Mother . . .

"And just before she died she said the important thing. She said that it was her fault, twenty-two years ago, and that you, Chimal, were not to blame. Do you know what she could have meant by that?"

So she was dead. Yet he already felt so cut off from his life in the valley that the pain of it was not as great as he expected.

"Speak," the Master Observer commanded. "Do you know what she meant?"

"Yes, but I shall not tell you. Your threat of death does not frighten me."

"You are a fool. Tell me at once. Why did she say twenty-two years? Did her guilt have something to do with your birth?"

"Yes," Chimal said, surprised. "How did you know?"

The old man waved the question aside with an impatient movement of his hand. "Answer me now, and truthfully, for this is the most important question in all of your lifetime. Tell me—what was your father's name?"

There was silence then, and Chimal realized that all the men were leaning forward, intent on his answer, almost forgetting the weapons they carried. Why shouldn't he tell them? What did broken taboos matter now?

"My father was Chimal-popoca, a man from Zaachila."

The words struck the old man like a blow. He staggered back and two of the men rushed to help him, dropping their weapons. The third man looked on, worried, with his own weapon and Chimal's killing thing both pointing downward. Chimal tensed himself to spring, grab one of them, and escape.

"No . . ." the Master Observer said hoarsely. "Observer Steadfast, drop those weapons at once."

As he had been ordered, the man bent and put them on the floor. Chimal took one step toward the door and stopped. "What does all this mean?" he asked.

The old man pushed his assistants away and made some adjustment on one of the devices suspended from his belt. His metal harness instantly stiffened and supported him, holding his head high.

"It means we welcome you, Chimal, and ask you to join s. This is a glorious day, one that we never expected to e in our lifetimes. The faithful will gain strength by touching you, and you will aid us to gain wisdom."

"I do not know what you are talking about," Chimal said desperately.

"There is much to tell you, so it is best to begin at the beginning . . ."

"What do these stars mean, *that* is what I want to know?"

The old man nodded, and almost smiled. "Already you teach us, for that is the beginning, you divined that." The others nodded. "That is the universe out there, and those stars are the ones the priests taught you about, for what they taught you was true."

"About the gods as well? There is no truth in those stories."

"Again you divine truth, unaided. Proof of your birthright. No, the false gods do not exist, except as stories for the simple to order their lives. There is only the Great Designer who did all this. I talk not of the gods, but of the other things you learned at the priests' school."

Chimal laughed. "About the sun being a ball of burning gas? I myself have seen the sun pass close and have touched the tracks it rides upon."

"That is true, but unknown even to them, this world we live in is not the world they teach about. Listen and it shall be revealed. There is a sun, a star just like any of those stars out there, and about it in eternal circle moves the Earth. We are all of that Earth, but have left it for the greater glory of the Great Designer." The others murmured response and touched their deuses at the words.

"It is not without reason we sing His praises. For look you, at what He has done. He has seen the other worlds that circle about the sun, and the tiny ships that men built to span those distances. Though these ships are fast, faster than we can possibly dream, they take weeks and months to go from planet to planet. Yet these distances are small compared to the distance between suns. The fastest of these ships would take a thousand years to travel to the nearest star. Men knew this and abandoned hope of traveling to other suns, to see the wonders of new worlds spinning about these distant flames.

"What weak man could not do, the Great Designer did. He did build this world and send it traveling to the star . . ."

"What are you saying?" Chimal asked, a sudden spurt of fear—or was it joy?—striking within him.

"That we are voyagers in a world of stone that is hurtling through emptiness, from star to star. A great ship for crossing the impalable waters of space. It is a hollow world, and in its heart is the valley, and in the valley live the Aztecs, and they are the passengers aboard the ship. Because the time has not yet come, the voyage itself is an unrevealed mystery for them, and they live out their happy lives in comfort and ease under a benevolent sun. To guard them and guide them we exist, the Watchers, and we fulfill our trust."

As though to underscore his words a great bell sounded once, then once again. The observers raised their deuses, and on the third stroke pressed down on the rods to add a number.

"And thus one more day of the voyage is done," the Master Observer intoned, "and we are one day closer to the Day of Arrival. We are true for all the days of our years."

"The days of our years," the others said in muted echo.

"Who am I?" Chimal asked. "Why am I different?"

"You are the child we have sworn to serve, the very reason for our being. For it is not written that the children shall lead them? That the Day of Arrival will come and the barrier will fall and the people of the valley shall be set free. They will come here and see the stars and know the truth at last. And on that day Coatlicue shall be destroyed before them and they shall be told to love one another, and that marriage between the clans of one village is forbidden and marriage is only proper between a man of one village and a woman of the other."

"My mother and father . . ."

"Your mother and father who entered grace too early and brought forth a true child of Arrival. In His wisdom the Great Designer put a blessing upon the Aztecs to remain humble and plant their crops and live their lives happily within the valley. This they do. But upon the day of arrival this blessing will be lifted and their children will do things their parents never dreamed possible, will read the books that are waiting and they will be ready to leave the valley forever."

Of course! Chimal did not know how it had been done,

101

but he knew that the words were true. He alone had not accepted the valley, had rebelled against the life there, had wanted to escape it. *Had* escaped it. He was different, he had always known it and been ashamed of it. That was no longer true. He stood straighter and looked around at the others.

"I have many questions to ask."

"They will be answered, all of them. We will tell you all we know and then you will learn more in the places of learning that are awaiting you. You, then, shall teach us."

Chimal laughed out loud at that. "Then you no longer want to kill me?"

The Master Observer lowered his head. "That was my mistake and I can only plead ignorance and ask forgiveness. You may kill me if you wish."

"Do not die so quickly, old man, you have many things to tell me first."

"That is true. Then—let us begin."

2

"What is it?" Chimal asked, looking apprehensively at the steaming, brown slab of meat on the plate before him. "There is no animal that I know that is big enough to provide this much meat." The suspicious look he gave the Master Observer inferred that he suspected which was the only animal large enough to supply it.

"It is called a beefsteak, and is particularly fine cut that we eat only on holidays. You may have it every day if you wish, the meatbank can supply enough."

"I know of no animal named a meatbank."

"Let me show you." The Master Observer made an adjustment on the televison set on the wall. His private quarters had none of the efficient starkness of the watchmen's cells. Here was music from some hidden source, there were paintings upon the walls and a deep carpet on the floor. Chimal, scrubbed clean and beardless after rubbing on a depilatory cream, sat in a soft chair, with many eat ing utensils and different dishes set before him. And th cannibalistically large piece of meat.

"Describe your work," the Master Observer said to the man who appeared on the screen. The man bowed his head.

"I am a Refection Tender, and the greatest part of my work is devoted to the meatbank." He stepped aside and pointed at the large vat behind him. "In the nutrient bath here grow certain edible portions of animals, placed here by the Great Designer. Nutrients are supplied, the tissues grow continually and pieces are trimmed off for our consumption."

"In a sense these pieces of animal are eternal," Chimal said when the screen had darkened. "Though part is removed, they never die. I wonder what the animal was?"

"I have never considered the eternal aspects of the meatbank. Thank you. I will now give it much thought because it seems an important question. The animal was called a cow, that is all I know about it."

Chimal hesitantly ate one bite, then more and more. It was better than anything he had ever tasted before. "The only thing missing are the chillies," he said, half aloud.

"There will be some tomorrow," the Master Observer said, making a note.

"Is this the meat you give to the vultures?" Chimal said, in sudden realization.

"Yes. The less desirable pieces. There is not enough small game in the valley to keep them alive, so we must supplement their diet."

"Why have them at all, then?"

"Because it is written, and is the Great Designer's way."

This was not the first time that Chimal had received this answer. On the way to these quarters he had asked questions, was still asking questions, and nothing was held back from him. But many times the Watchers seemed as unknowing about their destinies as the Aztecs. He did not voice this suspicion aloud. There was so much to learn!

"That takes care of the vultures," he had a sudden memory of a wave of death washing toward him, "but why the rattlesnakes and scorpions? When Coatlicue entered the cave a number of them came out. Why?"

"We are the Watchers and we must be stern in our duty. If a father has too many children he is not a good father, because he cannot provide for them all and therefore they go hungry. It is the same with the valley. If there were too many people, there would not be enough food for all. Therefore when the population exceeds a certain number of people of both sexes, worked out on a chart kept for that purpose, more snakes and insects are permitted to enter the valley."

"That's terrible! You mean those poisonous things are raised just to kill the people?"

"The correct decision is sometimes the hard one to make. That is why we are all taught to be strong and steadfast and to hew to the plan of the Great Designer."

There was no immediate answer to that. Chimal ate and drank the many good things before him and tried to digest what he had learned so far. He pointed his knife at the row of books across the room.

"I've tried to read your books, but they are very difficult and many of the words I don't know. Aren't there simpler books someplace?"

"There are, and I should have thought of it myself. But I am an old man and my memory is not as good as it should be."

"May I ask . . . just how old are you?"

"I am entering my one hundred and ninetieth year. As the Great Designer wills, I hope to see my full two hundred."

"Your people live so much longer than mine. Why is that?"

"We have much more to do in our lifetimes than simple farmers, therefore our years are the reward of our service. There are machines that aid us, and the drugs, and our eskoskeletons support and protect us. We are born to serve, and the longer that life of service, the more we can do."

Once again Chimal thought about this, but did not speak his thoughts. "And the books you were talking about . . . ?"

"Yes, of course. After today's service I will take you there. Only Observers are allowed, those who wear the red."

"Is that why I am wearing these red clothes as well?"

"Yes. It seemed wisest. It is the best, and most suitable for the First Arriver, and all the people will respect you."

"While you are at the service I would like to see t̄
104

place where the watchmen are, where they can see into the valley."

"We will go now, if you are ready. I will take you myself."

It was a different sensation to walk these tunnels without fear. Now, in his red clothing with the Master Observer at his side, all doors were open to him and the people saluted when they passed. Watchman Steel was waiting for them at the entrance to the observation center.

"I want to ask forgiveness," she said, eyes downcast. "I did not know who you were."

"None of us knew, Watchman," the Master Observer said, and reached out to touch her deus. "Yet that does not mean we should avoid penance, because an unconscious sin is still a sin. You will wear a mortification, thirty days, and come to love it."

"I do," she said fervently, hands clasped and eyes wide. "Through pain comes purification."

"May the Great Designer bless you," the old man said, then hurried away.

"Will you show me how you work?" Chimal asked.

"I thank you for asking me," the girl answered.

She led him into a large, circular, high-domed room that had screens inset into the wall at eye level. Watchmen sat before the screens, listening through earphones and occasionally talking into microphones that hung before their lips. Another raised observation station was in the center of the room.

"The Master Watchman sits there," Steel said, pointing. "He organizes the work of us all and guides us. If you will sit here I will show you what to do."

Chimal sat at an empty station and she pointed out the controls.

"With these buttons you choose the pickup you wish to use. There are 134 of them, and each one has a code and a watchman must know every code for instant response. They take years to learn because they must be perfect. Would you care to look?"

"Yes. Is there a pickup at the pond below the falls?"

"There is. Number 67." She tapped the buttons and the pool appeared, seen from behind the falls. "To hear, we o this." Another adjustment and the splashing of water as clear in his headphone, and the song of a bird belled

105

out from the trees. The image was sharp and in color, almost as though he were looking through a window in the rock at the valley outside.

"The pickup is mounted on the valley wall—or inside of it?" he asked.

"Yes, that is where most of them are so they will not be detected. Though of course there are many concealed inside the temples, such as this." The pool vanished and Itzcoatl appeared, pacing on the broad steps of the pyramid below the temple. "He is the new first priest. As soon as he was officially declared so, and had made the proper prayers and sacrifices, we permitted the sun to rise. The Sun Tenders say that they always welcome a chance to stop the sun for a day. It is a good chance to overhaul and adjust it."

Chimal worked the controls, picking numbers at random and feeding them into the machine. There appeared to be pickups all around the valley walls, and even one set into the sky above that gave a panoramic view of the entire valley. It could be turned and had a magnifying attachment that could bring the valley floor very close and clear, though of course there was no sound with the picture.

"There," Steel said, pointing at the image, "you can see the four high rocks that are along the river bank. They are too steep to be climbed . . ."

"I know, I have tried."

". . . and each one has a twin pickup on its summit. They are used to observe and control Coatlicue in the case of special circumstances."

"I had one of them on screen earlier," he said, pressing the buttons, "number 28. Yes, there it is."

"You remember that code very quickly," she said in awe. "I had to study many years."

"Show me some other things here, if you will," Chimal asked, rising.

"As you wish. Anything."

They went first to the refectory where one of the tenders insisted that they be seated and brought them warm drinks. The others had to help themselves to food.

"Everyone seems to know about me," he said.

"We were told at the morning service. You are the Fi‑

Arriver, there never has been one before, and everyone is very excited."

"What are we drinking?" he asked to change the subject, not enjoying the look of awe on her white face, the gaping mouth and slightly reddened nostrils.

"It is called tea. Do you find it refreshing?"

He looked around the large room, filled with the murmur of voices and the rattle of eating utensils, and suddenly realized something. "Where are the children? I don't think I have seen one anywhere."

"I do not know anything about that," she said, and her face was, if possible, whiter. "If there are any they must be in the place of the children."

"You don't know? That's a strange answer. Have you ever been married yourself, Watchman Steel? Do you have any children?"

Her face was bright red now, and she gave a small muffled cry as she sprang to her feet and ran from the refectory.

Chimal finished his tea and returned to find the Master Observer waiting for him. He explained what had happened and the old man nodded gravely.

"We can discuss it, since all things are guided by the observers, but the watchmen feel soiled by this kind of talk. They lead lives of purity and sacrifice and are far above the animal relationships that exist in the valley. They are Watchers first, women second, or women never for the most faithful ones. They weep because they were born with female bodies which embarrass them and hamper their vocation. Their faith is strong."

"Obviously. I hope you won't mind my asking—but your Watchers must come from someplace?"

"There are not many of us and we lead long and useful lives."

"I'm sure of that. But unless you live forever you are going to need new recruits. Where do they come from?"

"The place of the children. It is not important. We can go now." The First Observer rose to leave, but Chimal was not through yet.

"And what is at that place? Machines that make full grown children?"

"I sometimes wish there were. My hardest task is the
107

controlling of the place of the children. There is no order. There are four mothers there now, though one will die soon. These are women who have been chosen because, well, they did not do satisfactory work in their studies and could not master their assignments. They became mothers."

"And the fathers?"

"The Great Designer himself has ordered that. A frozen sperm bank. The technicians know how to use it. Great are His mysteries. Now, we must leave."

Chimal knew that was all he would hear at this time. He dropped the subject but did not forget it. They retraced the route they had taken when he had come here, after the observers had seen the alarm and gone to capture him. Through the great hall and down the golden corridor. The Master Observer pushed open one of the doors and showed him inside.

"It has been here since the beginning, waiting. You are the first. Simply sit in the chair before the screen and you will be shown."

"You will stay with me?"

For the first time the old man's down-tilting mouth curved reluctantly into a resigned smile. "Alas, that is not to be. This place is for arrivers only. It is my faith and my duty to tend it for them so it will always be ready." He went out and the door closed behind him.

Chimal sat in the comfortable chair and looked for a switch to start the machine, but this was not necessary. His weight in the chair must have actuated the device because the screen lit up and a voice filled the room.

"Welcome," the voice said. "You have come to Proxima Centauri."

EROS, one of the many asteroids in the asteroid belt, an area of planetary debris between the orbits of Mars and Jupiter, though there are violations to this rule. Eros is the most exceptional, with its orbit almost reaching that of Earth's at one point. Eros, cigar shaped, twenty miles long, solid rock. Then the plan. The greatest plan executed by mankind in a history of great plans, orginated by th man first called the Great Ruler now, truly, the Gre Designer. Who else but He could have conceived o' project that would take sixty years to prepare—and five hundred years to complete?

Eros, swinging close to Earth to receive its new destiny. Tiny ships, tinier men, jump the gap of airless space to begin this mighty work. Deep inside the rock they drill to first prepare their quarters, for many will live out their lives here, then further in to hollow out the immense chamber that will house a dream . . .

FUEL TANKS, filling them alone takes sixteen years. What is the mass of a mountain twenty miles long? Mass, it will supply its own reaction mass, and the fuel will eject that mass and someday it will move, out and away from the sun that it has circled for billions of years, never to return . . .

THE AZTECS, chosen after due consideration of all the primitive tribes of Earth. Simple people, self sufficient people, rich in gods, poor in wealth. Still, to this day, there are lost villages in the mountains, accessible only by footpath, where they live as they did when the Spaniards first arrived hundreds and hundreds of years earlier. One crop, corn, consuming most of their time and supplying most of their food. Vegetarians for the most part, with a little meat and fish when it is available. Brewing a hallucinatory drink from the maguey, seeing a god or a spirit in everything. Water, trees, rocks, all have souls. A pantheon of gods and goddesses without equal; Tezcatlipoca lord of Heaven and Earth, Mixtec lord of death, Mictla-tecuhtli lord of the dead. Hard work, warm sun, all-pervading religion, the perfect and obedient culture. Taken, unchanged, and set down in this valley in a mountain in space. Unchanged in all details, for who can guarantee what gives a culture adhesion—or what, if taken away, will bring it down? Taken whole and planted here, for it must continue unchanged for five hundred years. Some small truths added, minor alterations it is hoped will not destroy it. Writing. Basic cosmology. These are needed when the Aztecs finally emerge from the valley and their children take up their destiny.

DNA CHAINS, complex intertwined helixes with infinite permutations. Builders of life, controllers of life, with every detail from the hair on the leg to the flea on the body of the twenty ton whale locked into their convolutions. Billions of years developing, unraveled in short centuries. Is this the code for red hair? Replace it with that and the child will have black hair. Gene surgery, gene selection, delicate operations with the smallest building blocks of life, rearranging, ordering, producing . . .

GENIUS, exceptional natural capacity for creative and original conceptions, high intelligence quotient. Natural capacity, that means in the genes, and DNA. In a world population there are a goodly number of geniuses in every generation, and their DNA can be collected. And combined to produce children of genius. Guaranteed. Every time. Unless this genius is masked. For every capacity and condition in the genes there is a dominant and a recessive. Father dog is black and black is dominant and white is recessive, and he has that too. Mother is all black too. So they are BW and BW and, as the good Mendell taught, these factors can be plotted on the square named after him. If there are four pups they will be BB, BW, BW and WW, or a white dog where none was before. But is it possible to take a dominant and make it artificially recessive? Yes, it is possible. Take genius, for instance. They did take genius. And they tied it down to stupidity. Dimness. Subnormality. Passivity. Prison it in slightly different ways in two different groups of people and keep them apart. Let them have children, generation after generation of obedient, accepting children. And each child will carry that tied-down dominant, untouched and waiting. Then, some day, the right day, let the two groups meet and mingle and marry. The bonds are then released. The tied-down dominant is no longer recessive, it is dominant. The children are—children of different parents than their parents? Yes, perhaps they are. They are genius children.

There was so much to be learned. At any point in th recorded lecture Chimal could press the question butto and the pictures and voices would halt while the machine printed a list of references about the material then being covered. Some of these were recorded visual lectures that the viewer would play for him, others were specific volumes in the library. The library itself was a galaxy unexplored. Most of the books were photorecordings, though there were bound volumes of all the basic reference texts. When his head and his eyes ached from too much study and concentration, he would go through the library at random, picking up volumes and flicking through their pages. How complex the human body: the transparent pages of the anatomy text turned one by one to reveal the organs in vivid color. And the stars, they were giant burning spheres of gas after all, for here were charts with their temperatures and sizes. Page after page of photographs of nebulae, clusters, gas clouds. The universe was gigantic beyond comprehension—and he had once thought it was made of solid rock!

Leaving the astronomy book open on the table before him, Chimal leaned back and stretched, then rubbed at the soreness around his eyes. He had brought a thermos of tea with him and he poured a cup and sipped at it. The book had fallen open to a plate of the Great Nebula in Andromeda, a gigantic wheel of light against the star-pricked night. Stars. There was one star he should be interested in, the one he had been welcomed to when the process of education began. What was its name?—there were so many new things to remember—Proxima Centauri. It would still be far ahead, but he had a sudden desire to see the destination of his captive universe. There were detailed star charts of the sky, he had seen them, so it should not be too hard to pick out this individual star. And he could stretch his legs: his body ached from unaccustomed sitting for so many hours at a time.

It was a relief to walk briskly again, even run a few paces down the long passageway. How many days had it been since he had first entered the observation room? Memory fogged; he had kept no record. Maybe he should carry a deus like the others, but that was a bloody and painful way to mark the passing of a day. This rite seemed senseless to him, like so much of the Watchers' activities, but it was important to them. They seemed to actually enjoy this ritual infliction of pain. Once more he pushed

111

open the massive doors and looked out at interstellar space, as boldly impressive as the first time he had seen it.

Matching the stars to the chart was difficult. For one thing the stars did not remain in relatively fixed positions as they did in the sky above the valley, but instead swept by in majestic parade. In a few minutes the cycle would go from summer to winter constellations and back again. As soon as he thought he had plotted a constellation it would vanish from sight and new stars would appear. When the Master Observer came in he was grateful for the interruption.

"I regret having to bother you . . ."

"No, not at all, I'm getting nowhere with this chart and it only makes my head ache more."

"Then, might I ask you to aid us?"

"Of course. What is it?"

"You will see at once if you will accompany me."

The Master Observer's face was pulled into deeper lines of brooding seriousness: Chimal had not thought this was possible. When he tried to make conversation he received courteous but brief answers. Something was bothering the old man, and just what it was he would find out shortly.

They went downstairs to a level that Chimal had never visited and found a car waiting for them. It was a long ride, longer than he had ever taken before, and it was made in silence. Chimal looked at the walls moving steadily by and asked, "Are we going far?"

The Master Observer nodded. "Yes, to the stern, near the engine room."

Though Chimal had studied diagrams of their world, he still thought of it in relation to his valley. What they called the bow was where the observation room was, well beyond the swamp. The stern, then, was south of the waterfall, at the end of the valley. He wondered what they would find there.

They stopped at another tunnel opening and the Master Observer led the way to one of a number of identical doorways, outside of which was waiting a red-garbed observer. Silently, he opened the door for them. Inside was a sleeping cell. A man in Watcher's black was hanging from a rope that had been passed through the bar of the air vent in the ceiling. The loop of rope about his neck had choked him to death, slowly and painfully, rather than snapping his spine, but in the end it had done its job. He must have been hanging for days because his body had stretched so that his toes almost touched the floor, next to the overturned chair that he had jumped from. The observers turned away, but Chimal, no stranger to death, looked on calmly enough.

"What do you want me to do?" Chimal asked. For a moment he wondered if he had been brought as a burial party.

"He was the Air Tender and he worked alone because the Master Air Tender died recently and a new one has not been appointed as yet. His breviary is there on the desk. There seems to be something wrong and he was unable to correct it. He was a foolish man and instead of reporting it he took his own life."

Chimal picked up the well-thumbed and grease-stained book and flipped through it. There were pages of diagrams, charts for entering readings, and simple lists of instructions to be followed. He wondered what had troubled the man. The Master Observer beckoned him into the next room where a buzzer sounded continuously and a red light flashed on and off.

"This is a warning that something is wrong. The Air Tender's duty when the alarm sounds is to make the corrections at once, and then to make a written report to me. I received no such report."

"And the alarm is still going. I have a strong suspicion that your man could not fix the trouble, panicked and killed himself."

The Master Observer nodded in intensified gloom. "The same unharmonious thought is what came upon me when a report reached me that this had happened. I have been worried ever since the Master Air Tender was struck down in his youth, barely 110 years old, and this other one left in charge. The Master never thought well of him and we were preparing to train a new tender when this happened."

Chimal suddenly realized what this meant. "Then you have nobody who knows anything about repairing this equipment? And it is the air machinery you are talking about, that supplies the breathing air for us all?"

"Yes," the Master Observer said and led the way

through thick, double-locked doors to a vast and echoing chamber.

Tall tanks lined the walls with shining apparatus at their bases. Heavy ducts dived down and there was an all-pervading hum and the whine of motors.

"This supplies the air for everyone?" Chimal asked.

"No, nothing like that. You will read about it there, but most of the air has something to do with green plants. There are great chambers of them in constant growth. This apparatus does other important things with the air, just what I am not sure."

"I can't promise that I'll be able to help, but I'll do my best. At the same time I suggest you get whoever else might be able to work with this."

"There is no one, of course. No man would think of doing other than his assigned work. I alone am responsible and I have looked at this book before. Many of the things are beyond me. I am an old man, too old to learn a new discipline. A young man is now being taught the air tender's craft, but it will be years before he is able to work in here. That may be too late."

With a new weight of responsibility Chimal opened the book. The first part was an outline of air purification theory which he skimmed over quickly. He would read that in detail after he had a more general knowledge of the function of the machinery. Under *apparatus* there were 12 different sections, each headed with a large red number. These numbers were repeated on large signs down the wall and he assumed, with some justification, that they related to the numbers in the book. When he glanced up at them he noticed that a red light under 5 was blinking on and off. He walked over to it and saw the word *emergency* printed under the bulb: he opened the book to section 5.

"*Purification Tower, Trace Pollutants.* Many things such as machinery, paint and the breath of living people give off gaseous and particulate matter. There are not many of these pollutants, but they do collect over the years and can become concentrated. This machine removes from our air those certain fractions that may be dangerous after many, many years. Air is forced through a chemical that absorbs them . . ."

Chimal read on, interested now, until he had finished section 5. This tower seemed to be designed to function

114

for centuries without attention; nevertheless provision had still been made to have it watched and monitored. There was a bank of instruments at its base and he went to look at them. Another light was flashing over a large dial, blinking letters that spelled out REPLACE CHEMICAL. Yet on the dial itself the reading was right at the top of the activity scale, just where the book said it should be for correct operation.

"But who am I to argue with this machine," Chimal told the Master Observer, who had been following him in silence. "The recharging seems simple enough. There is an automatic cycle that the machine does when this button is depressed. If it doesn't work the valves can be worked by hand. Let's see what happens." He pushed the button.

Operation lights flashed on, flickering in response to the cycle, and hidden switches closed. A muffled, sighing sound issued from the column before them and, at the same time the needle on the activity scale moved into the red danger zone, dropping toward the bottom. The Master Observer squinted at it, spelling out the letters with his lips, then looked up, horrified.

"Can this be right? It gets worse not better. Something terrible is happening."

"I don't think so," Chimal said, frowning in concentration over the breviary. "It says the chemical needs replacing. So first I imagine the old chemical is pumped out, and this removal is what gives that false reading on the scale. Certainly the absence of a chemical will give the same reading as a bad chemical."

"Your argument is abstract, hard to follow. I am glad you are here with us, First Arriver, and I can see the workings of the Great Designer in this. We could do nothing about this without you."

"Let's see how this comes out, first. So far I've just followed the book and there has been no real problem. There, the new chemical must be coming in, the needle's going back up again to fully charged. That seems to be all there is to it."

The Master Observer pointed, horrified, at the blinking warning light. "Yet—that goes on. There is something terrible here. There is something wrong with our air!"

"There is nothing wrong with our air. But there is something wrong with this machine. It has been recharged, the new chemical is working perfectly—yet the alarm goes on. The only thing I can think of is that there is something wrong with the alarm." He slipped through the sections of the book until he found the one he wanted, then read through it quickly. "This may be it. Is there a storeroom here? I want something called 167-R."

"It is this way."

The storeroom contained rows of shelves, all numbered in order, and Chimal had no trouble locating part 167-R which was a sturdy cannister with a handle on the end and a warning message printed in red. CONTAINS PRESSURIZED GAS—POINT AWAY FROM FACE WHEN OPENING. He did as it advised and turned the handle. There was a loud hissing, and when it had died away the end came free in his hand. He reached in and drew out a glittering metal box, shaped like a large book. It had a handle where the spine would be and a number of copper-colored studs on the opposite edge. He had not the slightest idea what its function might be.

"Now let's see what this does."

The breviary directed him to the right spot and he found the handle in the face of the machine that was marked 167-R, as was the new one he had just obtained. When he pulled on the handle the container slid out as easily as a book from a shelf. He threw it aside and inserted the new part in its place.

"The light is gone, the emergency is over," the Master Observer called out in a voice cracking with emotion. "You have succeeded even where the Air Tender failed."

Chimal picked up the discarded part and wondered what had broken inside it. "It seemed obvious enough. The machinery appeared to work fine, so the trouble had to be in the alarm circuit, here. It's described in the book, in the right section. Something turned on and would not turn off, so the emergency sounded even after the correction had been made. The tender should have seen that."

He must have been very stupid not to have figured it out, he continued, to himself. Do not speak ill of the dead, but it was a fact. The poor man had panicked and killed himself when the problem had proven insoluble. This was proof of what he had suspected for a long time now.

In their own way the Watchers were just as slow-witted as the Aztecs. They had been fitted to a certain function just as the people in the valley had.

"I'm sorry, but I still don't understand it," Watchman Steel said, frowning over the diagram on the piece of paper, turning it around in the futile hope that a different angle would make everything clear.

"I'll show you another way then," Chimal said, going into his ablutory for the apparatus he had prepared. His observer's quarters were large and well appointed. He brought out the plastic container to which he had fastened a length of strong cord. "What do you see in here?" he asked, and she dutifully bent to look.

"Water. It is half filled with water."

"Correct. Now what will happen if I should turn it on its side?"

"Why . . . the water would spill out. Of course."

"Correct!"

She smiled happily at her success. Chimal stretched out a length of cord and picked up the container by it. "You said it would spill. Would you believe that I can turn this bucket on its side without spilling a drop?"

Steel just gaped in awe, believing anything possible of him. Chimal began to spin the bucket in a small circle, faster and faster, lifting it at the same time, until it was swinging in a circle straight up into the air, upside down at the summit of its loop. The water stayed in; not a drop was spilled. Then, slowly, he decreased the speed, until the container was once again on the floor.

"Now, one more question," he said, picking up a book. "If I were to open my hand and let go of this book—what would happen?"

"It would fall to the floor," she told him, intensely proud to have answered so many questions correctly.

"Right again. Now follow closely. The force that pulls the book to the floor and one that holds the water in the bucket is the same force, and its name is centrifugal force. There is another force on large planets called gravity that seems to act the same way, though I do not understand it. The important thing to remember is that centrifugal force so holds us down, so we don't fly up into the air, and is also the reason why we could walk across the sky and look up at the valley over our heads."

"I don't understand any of that," she admitted.

"It's simple. Say that instead of a cord I had a spinning wheel. If the container were hung from the rim of the wheel the water would stay inside of it just as it did when I spun it on the cord. And I could fasten *two* containers to the wheel, opposite each other, and the water would stay in each one. The bottom of each container would be down for the water it held—yet the direction down would be *directly opposite* for each of them. The same thing is true for us, because this world of rock is spinning too. So *down* in the village is below your feet—and down on the sky is toward the sky. Do you follow all of this?"

"Yes," she told him, although she did not, but she wanted to please him.

"Good. Now the next step is the important one and I want you to be sure you are with me. If down is below your feet in the village and down is toward the sky when you are opposite it, then halfway between them the force must be equal, so that there is no force acting at all. If we could get halfway to the sky from the village we could just float there."

"That would be very hard to do, unless you were a bird. And even birds are prevented from leaving the valley by a certain device of which I have heard."

"Very true. We can't climb up through the air, but we can go through a tunnel in the rock. The valley is in an opening in the rock, but it is solid at both ends. If there is a tunnel leading to the spot, it's called the axis of rotation, that's the name from the book, we could go there and float in the air."

"I don't think I would like that."

"I would. And I have found the right tunnel on the charts. Will you go with me?"

Watchman Steel hesitated; she had no desire to experience adventures of this kind. But the First Arriver's wishes must be treated as law.

"Ye, I will come."

"Good. We'll go now." The books were satisfactory and he enjoyed his studies, but he needed human contact too. In the village people were always together. Watchman Steel was the first person he had met here, and they had shared experiences together. She was not bright, but sh tried to please. He put some food concentrates and a water bottle into his belt pouch: he had taken to wearing this as did all the others. It held the communicator, his writing instruments, some small tools.

"It's the second stairway past the refectory," he told her as they left.

At the foot of the stairway they stopped while she set her eskoskeleton for *climb*. It moved one foot after the other, providing all the power to lift her weight and therefore prevented undue strain on her heart. Chimal slowed down to match her mechanical pace. They went up seven levels before the stairway ended.

"This is the top level," Steel said as she reset the controls. "I have only been up here once before. There are just storerooms here."

"More than that, if the diagrams are correct."

They walked the length of the corridor, past the last doorway, and on through the drill-scored, chill rock. There was no heated flooring here, but their boots did have thick, insulated soles. At the very end, facing them, was a metal doorway with the painted legend in large, red letters: OBSERVERS ONLY.

"I can't go in there," she said.

"You can if I tell you to. In the observer's breviary it states that watchmen or anyone else may be ordered by observers into any area to do what is needed." He had never read anything of the sort, but she did not have to know that.

"Of course, then I can go with you. Do you know the combination of this lock?" She pointed at the complex dial lock that was fastened to the edge of the door on a hasp.

"No, there was nothing about there being a lock on this door."

This was the first sealed door that he had seen. Rule and order were enough to keep the Watchers from entering where they were not wanted. He looked closely at the lock, and at the hasp.

"This has been added after the original construction," he said, pointing to the screw heads. "Someone has drilled into the metal frame and door and attached this." He took out a screwdriver and twisted a screw loose. "And not a very good job either. They did not fix it very securely."

It took only a few moments to remove the retaining screws and put the lock, still sealed to the hasp, onto the tunnel floor. The door opened easily then, into a small, metal-walled room.

"What can this mean?" Steel asked, following him in.

"I'm not sure I know. There were no details on the charts. But—we can follow the instructions and see what happens." He pointed to the lettered card on one wall. "One, close door, that's simple enough. Two, hold fast to handgrips."

There were metal loops fixed to the walls at waist height, and they both took hold of them.

"Three, turn pointer in proper direction."

A metal arrow beneath the sign had its tip touching the word DOWN. It was pivoted on its base and Chimal released one hand to push the point of the arrow to UP. When he did so a distant humming began and the car began to move slowly upward.

"Very good," he said. "Saves us a long climb. This car must be fixed in a vertical shaft and is pulled up and down by a device of some kind. What's the matter?"

"I . . . I don't know," Steel gasped, clutching to the ring with both hands. "I feel so strange, different."

"Yes, you're right. Lighter perhaps!" He laughed and jumped up from the floor, and it seemed to take longer than usual before he dropped back. "The centrifugal force is decreasing. Soon it will be gone completely." Steel, not as enthused by the idea as he was, clasped tight and pressed her head to the wall with her eyes closed.

The trip was relatively brief, and, when the car stopped, Chimal pushed up on his toes and floated free of the floor.

"It's true—there is no force acting. We are at the axis of rotation." Steel curled over, gasping and retching, trying to control the spasms in her stomach. The door opened automatically and they looked along a circular corridor with rods, like raised rails, running the length of it. There was no up or down and even Chimal felt a little queasy when he tried to imagine in what direction they were facing.

"Come on. We just float, then pull ourselves along those rods to wherever the tunnel goes. It should be easy." When the girl showed no intention of moving he pried her hands loose and gently pushed her into the end of the tube, knocking himself back against the wall at the same time. She screamed faintly and thrashed about, trying to clutch onto something. He launched himself after her and discovered it was not easy at all.

In the end he found that the surest way to progress was to pull forward lightly, then guide himself by sliding his hands along the bar as he went. Watchman Steel, after emptying her stomach felt somewhat better and managed to follow his instructions. Bit by bit they progressed the length of the tube to the doorway at the end, then let themselves through into a spherical room that looked out onto the stars.

"I recognize that long instrument," Chimal said excitedly. "It's a telescope, for making far away things look bigger. It can be used for looking at the stars. I wonder what the other instruments do."

He had forgotten Steel, which she did not mind at all. There was a couch attached to one portion of the wall and she found that she could fix herself in it by tightening straps across her body. She did this and closed her eyes.

Chimal was almost unaware of the lack of any force pulling him down as he read the operating instructions on the machine. They were simple and clear and promised wonders. The stars outside of the bulging, hemispherical window, were rotating in slow circles about a point in the middle. Not as fast as the stars in the observation room, and they weren't rising or setting, but they were still moving. When he actuated a control, as instructed, he felt a sudden force pulling on him, the girl moaned, and the sensation quickly stopped. When he turned to look out of the doorway it looked as though the tunnel was now turning—and the stars were now still. The room must now be rotating in the opposite direction from the rest of the world, so they were motionless in relation to the stars. What wonders the Great Designer had created!

Once the computer was actuated it needed two points of reference. After it knew these it was self orientating. Following the instructions, Chimal pointed the pilot scope at a bright, glowing red star, fixed it in the crosshairs of the telescope, then pressed the spectrum analysis button. The identification was instantly projected on a small screen: Aldebaran. Not far away from it was another bright star that appeared to be in the constellation he knew as The Hunter. Its name was Rigel. Perhaps it was in The Hunter, it was so hard to tell even well-known constellations with the infinitude of lights that filled the sky.

"Look at it," he called to the girl, in pride and wonder.

"That is the real sky, the real stars." She looked quickly and nodded, and closed her eyes again. "Outside this window is space, vacuum, no air to breathe. Just nothing at all, an empty immensity. How can the distance be measured to a star—how can we imagine it? And this, this world of ours, is going from one star to another, will reach it some day. Do you know the name of the star that is our destination?"

"We were taught—but I'm afraid I have forgotten."

"Proxima Centauri. In an old language that means the closest star in the constellation of the centaur. Don't you want to see it? What a moment this is. It is one of those out there, right in front of us. The machine will find it."

Carefully, he set the dials for the correct combination, checking them twice to be sure he had entered the right numbers from the printed list. It was correct. He pressed the actuate button and moved back.

Like the snout of a great, questing animal the telescope shivered and swung slowly into motion. Chimal stayed clear as it turned with ponderous precision, slowed and stopped. It was pointing far to one side, almost 90 degrees from the center of the window.

Chimal laughed. "That can't be," he said. "There has been a mistake. If Proxima Centauri were way over there, out to the side, it would mean that we were going past it . . ."

His fingers shook as he returned to the list and checked his figures over and over again.

4

"Just look at these figures and tell me if they are true or not—that's all I ask." Chimal dropped the papers onto the table before the Master Observer.

"I have told you, I am not very practiced at the mathematics. There are machines for this sort of thing." The old man stared straight ahead, looking neither at the papers nor at Chimal, unmoving except for his fingers that plucked, unnoticed, at his clothing.

"These are from a machine, a readout. Look at ther

and tell me if they are correct or not."

"I am no longer young and it is time for prayers and rest. I ask you to leave me."

"No. Not until you have given me an answer. You don't want to answer, do you?"

The old man's continued silence destroyed the last element of calmness that Chimal possessed. The Master Observer gave a hoarse cry as Chimal reached out to seize his deus and, with a quick snap, broke the chain that supported it. He looked at the numbers in the openings in the front.

"186,293 . . . do you know what that means?"

"This is—close to blasphemy. Return that, at once."

"I was told that this numbered the days of the voyage, days in old Earth time. As I remember it there are about 365 days in an Earth year."

He threw the deus onto the table and the old man snatched it up at once, in both hands. Chimal took a writing tablet and a stylus from his belt. "Divide . . . this shouldn't be hard . . . the answer is . . ." He scrawled a line under the figure and waved it under the Master Observer's nose. "It's been over 510 years since the voyage began. The estimate in all the books was five hundred years or less, and the Aztecs believe they will be freed in 500 years. This is just added evidence. With my own eyes I saw that we are no longer going toward Proxima Centauri, but are aimed instead almost at the constellation Leo."

"How can you know that?"

"Because I was in the navigation chamber and used the telescope. The axis of rotation is no longer pointing at Proxima Centauri. We are going somewhere else."

"These are all very complex questions," the old man said, dabbing a kerchief at the corners of his red-rimmed eyes. "I remember no relationship between the axis of rotation and our direction. . . ."

"Well I do—and I have checked already to make sure. To keep the navigational instruments functioning correctly, Proxima Centauri is fixed at the axis of rotation. Automatic course corrections are made if it drifts—so we move in the direction of the main axis. This cannot be changed." Chimal chewed at a knuckle in sudden thought. Though we might now be going to a different star! Now ll me the truth—what has happened?"

The old observer stayed rigid for a moment longer, then collapsed, sighing, inside the restraining support of his eskoskeleton.

"There is nothing that can be kept from you, First Arriver, I realize that now. But I did not want you to know until you had come to full knowledge. That must be now, or you would not have found out these things." He threw a switch and the motors hummed as they lifted him to his feet and moved him across the room.

"The meeting is recorded here in the log. I was a young man at the time, then the youngest observer in fact, the others are long since dead. How many years ago was that? I am not sure, yet I still remember every detail of it. An act of faith, an act of understanding, an act of trust." He seated himself again, holding a red bound book in both hands, looking at it, through it, to that well remembered day.

"We were weeks, months almost, weighing all of the facts and coming to a decision. It was a solemn, almost heart-stopping moment. The Chief Observer stood and read all of the observations. The instruments showed that we had slowed, that new data must be fed in to put us into an orbit about the star. Then he read about the planetary observations and we all felt distress at what had been discovered. The planets were not suitable, that was what was wrong. Just not suitable. We could have been the Observers of the Day of Arrival, yet we had the strength to turn away from the temptation. We had to fulfill the trust of the people in our charge. When the Master Observer explained this we all knew what had to be done. The Great Designer had planned even for this day, for the chance that no satisfactory planets could be found in orbit about Proxima Centauri, and a new course was set to Alpha Centauri. Or was it Wolf 359 in Leo? I forget now, it had been so many years. But it is all in here, the truth of the decision. Hard as it was to make—it was made. I shall carry the memory of that day with me to the recycler. Few are given such a chance to serve."

"May I see the book? What day was this decided?"

"A day fixed in history, but look for yourself." The old man smiled and opened the book, apparently at random, on the table before him. "See how it opens to the correct place? I have read in it so often."

Chimal took the book and read the entry. It occupie

less than a page. Surely a record of brevity for such a momentous occasion.

"There is nothing here about the observations and the reasons for the decisions," he said. "No details on the planets that were so unsuitable."

"Yes, there, beginning the second paragraph. If you will permit me I can quote from memory. '. . . therefore, it was the observations alone that could determine future action. The planets were unsuitable.' "

"But why? There are no details."

"Details are not needed. This was a decision of faith. The Great Designer had made allowance for the fact that suitable planets might not be found, and He is the one who knew. If the planets were suitable he would have not given us a choice. This is a very important doctrinal point. We all looked through the telescope and agreed. The planets were not suitable. They were tiny, and had no light of their own like a sun, and were very far away. They obviously were not suitable . . ."

Chimal sprang to his feet, slamming the book onto the table.

"Are you telling me that you decided simply by looking through the telescope while still at astronomical distance? That you made no approaches, no landings, took no photographs . . . ?"

"I know nothing of those things. They must be things that Arrivers do. We could not open the valley until we were sure these planets were proper. Think—how terrible! What would it have been like if the Arrivers found these planets unsuitable! We would have betrayed our trust. No, far better to make this weighty decision ourselves. We knew what was involved. Every one of us searched his heart and faith before coming to a reluctant decision. The planets were unsuitable."

"And this was decided by faith alone?"

"The faith of good men, true men. There was no other way, nor did we want one. How could we have possibly erred as long as we stood true to our beliefs?"

In silence, Chimal copied the date of the decision onto his writing tablet, then put the book back onto the table.

"Don't you agree that it was the wisest decision?" the Master Observer asked, smiling.

"I think you were all mad," Chimal said.

"Blasphemy! Why do you say that?"

"Because you knew nothing at all about those planets, and a decision made without facts or knowledge is no decision—just superstitious nonsense."

"I will not hear these insults—even from the First Arriver. I ask you respectfully to leave my quarters."

"Facts are facts, and guesswork is guesswork. Stripped of all the mumbo-jumbo and faith talk, your decision is just baseless. Worse than a guess since you make a guess from incomplete facts. You pietistical fools had no facts at all. What did the rest of your people say about the decision?"

"They did not know. It was not their decision. They serve, that is all they ask. That is all we observers asked."

"Then I'm going to tell them all, and find the computer. We can still turn back."

The eskoskeleton hummed to follow his body as the old man stood, straight and angry, pointing his finger at Chimal.

"You cannot. It is forbidden knowledge for them and I forbid you to mention it to them—or to go near the computers. The decision of the observers cannot be reversed."

"Why not? You are just men. Damn fallible, stupid men at that. You were wrong and I'm going to right that wrong."

"If you do you will prove that you are not the First Arriver after all, but something else. I know not what. I must search the breviary for the meaning of this."

"Search, I act. We turn."

For long minutes after Chimal slammed out the Master Observer stood, staring at the closed door. When he finally reached a decision he wanted to groan aloud with unhappiness at the terribleness of it all. But hard decisions had to be made too: that was the burden of his responsibility. He picked up his communicator to make the call.

The sign on the door read NAVIGATION ROOM —OBSERVERS ONLY. Chimal had been so angry at the time of his discovery that he had not thought to search out this room and verify his information. The anger was still there, but now it was cold and disciplined: he would do whatever had to be done. A search of the charts had revealed the existence of this place. He pushed open the door and went in.

The room was small and contained only two chairs,

computer input, some breviaries of data, and a chart on the wall of simplified operating instructions. The input was designed for a single function and took instructions in ordinary language. Chimal read the chart quickly, then sat before the input and tapped out a message with one finger.

IS THE ORBIT NOW TOWARD PROXIMA CENTAURI?

As soon as he pressed the button for *answer* the input burst into rapid life and typed:

NO.

HAVE WE PASSED PROXIMA CENTAURI?

QUESTION IS UNCLEAR. SEE INSTRUCTION 13.

Chimal thought a moment, then fed in a new question.

CAN THE ORBIT BE CHANGED TO GO TO PROXIMA CENTAURI?

YES.

That was better. Chimal typed in HOW LONG WILL IT TAKE TO REACH PROXIMA CENTAURI IF THE ORBIT IS CHANGED NOW? This time the computer took almost three seconds to answer, since there were many computations to be made and memories to be consulted.

ESTIMATED ARRIVAL 100 ASTRONOMICAL UNITS DISTANCE PROXIMA CENTAURI 17,432 DAYS.

Chimal did the division quickly. "That's less than 50 years. The arrival might even be in my lifetime if we begin the new orbit now!"

But how? How could the observers be made to change the orbit? There was a possibility that he could find the proper instructions and breviaries and work out how to do it himself, but only if he were undisturbed. He could not possibly do the work in the face of their active hostility. Nor would words alone convince them. What would? They had to be forced to make the orbit change whether they wanted to or not. Violence? It wouldn't be possible to capture them all and force them to the work. The Watchers would never permit this. Nor could he simply kill them: this was equally distasteful, though he was certainly in the humor for it. He felt like doing violence to something.

The air machinery? The equipment he had worked on —it was vital for life, but only over a period of time. If re were some way to damage it, he was the only one

127

who would be able to repair it. And he would not even begin the repairs until the course had been changed and they were on their way to the nearby star.

This was what he had to do. He slammed out into the passageway and saw the Master Observer and the other observers hurrying toward him at the highest speed their eskoskeletons would go. Chimal ignored their shouts and ran in the opposite direction, easily outdistancing them. As fast as he could, by the most direct route, he ran to the tunnel that went to the air plant.

The track was empty. No car was waiting.

Should he walk? It would take hours to get through this tunnel that ran the full length of the valley. And if they sent a car after him there would be no possibility of escape. He needed a car himself—but should he call for one? If all the Watchers had been alerted he would be simply trapping himself. He had to make a decision quickly. It was a better than good chance that the people had not been informed; that was not the Master Observer's way. He turned to the communicator on the wall.

"This is the First Arriver. I want a car at once, at station 187." The speaker hummed silently for a moment, then a voice answered.

"It shall be as you order. It will be there in a few minutes."

Would it? Or would the man report it to the observers? Chimal paced in an agony of apprehension, unable now to do anything except wait. It was only a few minutes before the car arrived, but the time seemed endless to him.

"Would you wish me to drive?" the operator said.

"No, I can do it myself."

The man climbed out and saluted Chimal respectfully as the car started down the track. The way was clear. Even if the man did report him, Chimal knew that he had a clear lead. If he kept ahead of any possible pursuers and worked fast he should finish what he had to do before they caught up with him. But now, before he arrived, he must think ahead, plan what would be the best thing to do. The machinery was so massive it would take too long to injure any of that, but the control panels were smaller and more lightly made. Simply destroying some of the instruments or removing their components should be enough. The observers would never be able to repair them without his help. But before he broke anything he had to be sure tha

128

there were replacements. Simply removing components from the controls might not be enough; the Master Observer, if pressed, might be able to figure that out from the empty slots. No, something must be broken.

When the car slammed to a stop at the other end of the tunnel he jumped from it, every move planned in advance. First the breviary. It was resting just where he had left it. There was no one else here so apparently the new tender had not taken up his position yet. That was just as well. He had to find the correct diagram, then the parts numbers. He walked into the storeroom as he read. Yes, here they were, the readouts and mechanical actuators from the panel. More than ten of each. The Great Designer had planned well, and overprovided for every eventuality. But He had not considered sabotage. As an added precaution, Chimal removed all the replacements and took them to another storeroom where he buried them deep behind a stock of massive piping. Now, destruction.

A great, open-end wrench, heavy and as long as his arm, would make a perfect weapon. He took it into the main chamber and stood before the board, weighing it in both hands. There, the glass-faced pressure dial first. He swung the wrench up over his head like a war-ax and brought it down with a splintering crash.

Instantly red lights flashed on and off all over the chamber and a siren began a shrill, ear-hurting scream. An amplified voice, louder than thunder, roared out at him.

"STOP! STOP WHAT YOU ARE DOING! YOU ARE INJURING THE MACHINE! THIS IS THE ONLY WARNING YOU WILL HAVE!"

Flashing lights and warnings were not going to stop him. He brought the wrench down again on the same spot. As he did this a metal door burst open in the wall above him, showering down dust. The muzzle of a laser gun slammed out into position and began firing instantly, the green pencil of flame cutting an arc in front of the control panel.

Chimal threw himself aside but not quickly enough. The beam caught his left side, his leg, his arm, burning through the clothing instantly and deep into the flesh. He fell heavily, almost unconscious from the sudden shock and pain.

The Great Designer had considered everything, even the

possibility of sabotage, Chimal realized. Far too late.

When the observers hurried in they found him this way, crawling, leaving a painful track of blood. Chimal opened his mouth to say something but the Master Observer gestured and stepped aside. A man with a tank on his back and a gun-like nozzle in his hand moved forward and pressed the trigger. A cloud of gas engulfed Chimal and his head dropped heavily to the stone flooring.

5

While he was unconscious the machines cared for him. The observers stripped his clothes from him and placed him in the trough on the table. They fed in a description of his injuries, then let the analyzer decide for itself. Once begun the entire operation was completely automatic.

X-rays were taken, while his blood pressure, temperature and all other vital statistics were recorded. Blood clotting foam was applied at once to the wounds, as soon as they had been photographed. Diagnosis took place inside the computer and treatment was programmed. The analysis apparatus rose silently up into its container and a shining metallic surgeon took its place. It hovered over the wound while its binocular microscopes peered deep, its many arms ready. Although it worked on only a very small area at a time it worked incredibly fast, far faster than could any careful human surgeon, as it followed the program of the computer. A speck of foam was flicked away, the area cleaned, burned tissue removed in a lightning debridement. Then a binding glue, that accelerated tissue growth as well, was applied and the flashing instruments moved on. Down his arm, closing the wound, sewing the severed tendons, rejoining the cut nerve endings. Then to his side where the laser ray had cut deep into the muscles, although it had not touched any of the internal organs. Finally the leg, a burned area on his thigh, the simplest wound of all.

When Chimal awoke he had difficulty at first in remembering what had happened and why he was here in the hospital. He was heavily sedated and felt no pain, but head was light and he felt too exhausted to even roll over.

Memory returned, and with it bitterness. He had failed. The endless voyage to nowhere would go on. The observers were too faithful to their trust of preserving; they could not consider ending it. Perhaps the Great Designer had made His only mistake here by planning too well. The Watchers were so efficient at their work, and so pleased by it, that they could even consider the possibility of bringing it to a halt. The next star, if they ever reached it, would also be sure to have unsatisfactory planets. He had had only one chance to end the voyage, and Chimal had failed in the attempt. There would be no more chances for him, the observers would see to that—and there would be no more Chimals after this. The warning would be heeded. If any more children were ever born of a union between the two villages, they would not be welcome here. Perhaps the gods might even whisper in the first priest's ear and there would be a welcome sacrifice.

The nursing machines, aware that he had returned to consciousness, removed the intravenous feeding drip from his arm and produced a bowl of warm broth.

"Please open your mouth," the sweet, recorded voice of a girl, centuries dead, told him, and a bent tube was lowered into the broth and brought carefully to his lips. He obliged.

The machine must also have announced that he was awake because the door opened and the Master Observer came in.

"Why did you do this impossible thing?" he asked. "None of us can understand it. It will be months before the damage can be fixed since we cannot trust you near it again."

"I did it because I want you to change our orbit. I would do anything to make you do that. If we made the change now we could be near Proxima Centauri in less than fifty years. That's all I'm asking you to do, just look closer at the planets. You don't even have to promise to tell anyone other than the observers. Will you do it?"

"Now don't stop," the gentle voice chided. "You have to finish it all up, every drop. You hear?"

"No. Of course not. It is not up to me at all. The decision has been made and recorded and I cannot possibly think of changing it. You should not even ask me."

131

"I have to, to appeal to you—how? In the name of humanity? End the centuries of imprisonment and fear and death. Free your own people from the tyranny that controls them."

"What madness are you talking?"

"Truth. Look at my people, living brutalized, superstitious and short lives, their population controlled by venomous snakes. Monstrous! And your own morbid people, these poor women like Watchman Steel, a ghost of a self-torturing female with none of the normal traits of her sex. Loathing motherhood and loving to inflict pain upon herself. You can end the bondage of all of them . . ."

"Stop," the Master Observer commanded, raising his hand. "I will hear no more of this blasphemous talk. This world is a perfect world, just as the Great Designer ordered it, and to even speak of changing it is a crime beyond imagining. I have considered for many hours what to do with you, and have consulted with the other observers, and we have reached a decision."

"Kill me and shut me up forever?"

"No, we cannot do that. Warped as you are by your incorrect upbringing among the savages in the valley, you are still the First Arriver. Therefore you will arrive, that is our decision."

"What nonsense is this?" Chimal was too tired to argue more. He pushed the unemptied bowl away and shut his eyes.

"The diagrams disclose that there are five objects called spaceships in caverns on the outer skin of this world. They are described carefully and have been designed to travel from here to whatever planet is to be settled. You will be placed into one of these spaceships and you will leave. You will go to the planets as you wish. You will be the First Arriver."

"Get out," Chimal said, wearily. "No, you're not killing me, just sending me on a fifty year voyage by myself, in exile, alone for the rest of my life. In a ship that may not even carry enough food and air for a voyage of that length. Leave me, you filthy hypocrite."

"The machines inform me that in ten days you will b cured enough to leave this bed. An eskoskeleton is bei: prepared to aid you. At that time observers will come a see that you board the ship. They will drug you and ca

132

you if they must. You will go. I will not be there because I do not wish to see you again. I will not even say goodby because you have been a sore trial in my life, and have said blasphemous words that I will never forget. You are too evil to bear." The old man turned and left even before he was through speaking.

Ten days, Chimal thought, as he drifted on the edge of sleep. Ten days. What can I possibly do in that time? What can I possibly do at all? To end this tragedy. How I wish I could expose the indecency of the life these people lead. Even the lives of my people, short and unhappy as they are, are better than this. I would like to break open this termites' nest to their gaze, to let them see just what kind of people they are who hide and skulk nearby, watching and ordering.

His eyes opened wide and, unconscious of what he was doing, he sat bolt upright in the bed.

"Of course. Let my people into these caverns. There would be no choice then—we would have to change the orbit for Proxima Centauri."

He dropped back onto the pillows. He had ten days to make plans and decide just what to do.

Four days later the eskoskeleton was brought in and stood in a corner. During the next sleeping period he dragged himself from the bed and put it on, practicing with it. The controls were simple and foolproof. He was out of bed every night after that, tottering at first, then walking grimly in spite of the pain. Doing simple exercises. His appetite increased. The ten day figure was far more time than he needed. The machines must have estimated his period of healing by using as a standard the sluggish metabolisms of the Watchers. He could do much better than that.

There was always an observer on guard outside of his room, he heard them talking when they changed shifts, but they never entered. They wanted to have nothing to do with him. During the sleeping period of the ninth day Chimal rose and silently dressed himself. He was still weak, but the eskoskeleton helped that, taking most of the exertion out of walking and other physical movements. A ght chair was the only possible weapon that the room ovided. He took it in both hands and stood behind the or—then screamed.

133

"Help! I'm bleeding . . . I'm dying . . . help!"

At once he had to raise his voice and shout louder to drown out the voice of the nurse who kept ordering him back to bed for an examination. Surely alarms were going off somewhere. He had to be fast. Where was that fool of an observer? How long did it take him to make up his simple mind? If he didn't come in soon Chimal would have to go after him, and if the man were armed that could be dangerous.

The door opened and Chimal hit him with the chair as soon as he entered. He rolled on the floor and moaned but there was no time to even look at him. One man—or a world? Chimal pried the laser rifle from his fingers and went out, moving at the fastest speed the eskoskeleton would permit.

At the first turning he left the hospital passage and headed toward the outermost corridors, the ones that were usually deserted, almost certainly so at this hour. It was one hour to dawn, the Watchers of course kept the same time as the valley, and he would need every minute of that. The route he had planned was circuitous and he was so slow.

No one would know what he had planned, that certainly would help. Only the Master Observer could make decisions, and he did not make them easily. The first thing he would probably think of would be that Chimal might return to finish his job of sabotage. Weapons would be found and observers dispatched to the air plant. Then more thought. A search perhaps, and finally the alerting of all the people. How long would that take? Impossible to estimate. Hopefully more than an hour. If it happened sooner Chimal would fight. Hurt, kill if necessary. Some would die so that future generations might live.

The Master Observer moved even slower than Chimal imagined. Almost the entire hour had passed before he met another man, and this one was obviously bent on a routine errand. When he came close and recognized Chimal he was too shocked to do anything. Chimal got behind him and let the powered hands of the eskoskeleton throttle the man into unconsciousness. Now—dawn, and the last corridor.

His life was running backwards. This was the way h had entered, so long ago, going fearfully in the other dire

134

tion. How he had changed since that day: how much he had learned. Valueless things unless he could put them to some real use. He came down the stone-floored tunnel just as the door at the far end swung up and outward. Outlined against the blue of the morning sky stood the monstrous figure of Coatlicue, snake-headed and claw-armed. Coming toward him. In spite of knowledge his heart leapt in his chest. But he walked on, straight toward her.

The great stone swung silently shut again and the goddess came forward, gaze fixed and unseeing. She came up to him and past him—then turned and entered the niche to wheel about and stand, frozen and inactive. To rest for one more day before emerging on her nightly patrol.

"You are a machine," Chimal said. "Nothing more. And there, behind you, are tools and parts cabinets and your breviary." He walked past her and picked it up and read the cover. "And your name isn't even Coatlicue, it is HEAT SEEKING GUARD ROBOT. Which explains now how I escaped from you—once I was under the water I vanished as far as your senses were concerned." He opened the book.

Though the Coatlicue robot was undoubtedly complex, the repairs and instructions were simple, like all the others. Chimal had originally thought that it would be enough to open the portal and send her out in the daylight. But there was far more he could do with her. Following the directions he slid aside a panel in the machine's back and exposed a multiholed socket. In the cabinet was a control box with a length of wire and a matching plug. With this the automatic circuits could be over ridden and the machine tested and moved about at the will of the controller. Chimal plugged it in.

"Walk!" he commanded, and the goddess lurched forward.

"In a circle," he said and worked the controls. Coatlicue dutifully trundled in a circle about him, brushing against the cavern walls, her twisting heads just below the high ceiling.

He could lead her out and command her to do just what he wished. No—not lead! He could do far better than that.

"Kneel!" he shouted, and she obeyed. Laughing, he put e foot in her bent elbow and climbed to her shoulders

135

and sat, his heels dangling amid the dried human hands, while he held to one of her hard and metallically scaly necks.

"Now, forward, we are leaving. I am Chimal," he shouted. "The one who left and returned—and who rides a goddess!"

As they approached the exit it swung up in response to some automatic signal. He stopped the machine under the door and examined the mechanism. Heavy pistons pushed it open and held it that way. If he could melt the rods, bend them without destroying them, the door would be held rigidly open beyond quick repair. And what he had to do would not take too long. Not long indeed. The laser beam played over the smooth rod of the piston until it turned red and suddenly sagged under the weight of the rock. He turned the beam quickly away and the door fell. But it stopped quickly, still supported by the piston on the other side. The first one was bent, the metal firm again, and would not be able to move back into the cylinder in this damaged condition. The door was sealed open.

Out into the valley Chimal rode his strange mount, the snake heads and snake-kirtle hissing loudly, but not as loud as his victorious laughter.

As the trail emerged from the crevice Chimal stopped and looked across his valley with mixed feelings: he had not realized until this moment that he would enjoy being back. Home. There was still a dawn haze hanging over the fields along the river bed. This would burn away as soon as the sun cleared the mountains. He breathed deep of the clean, sharp air that was touched with the scent of green growing things. It was pleasant to be outdoors again after the musty deadness of the corridors. Yet, as he thought this, he realized that his valley was just a large cavern torn from solid rock, and while he looked at it he was also aware of the tunnels that surrounded it and the empty space and stars outside. These thoughts were disconcerting and he shivered and put them from his mind. His wounds ached; he had moved too much and too soon. He started the goddess ahead, down to the riverbank and across, splashing through the shallow water.

In the villages people would be washing now and preparing the morning meal. Soon they would be leaving fo the fields and if he hurried he would get there at the same time. A twist of the controls sent Coatlicue trundling forward at a slow run, jarring his body with every step. He closed his teeth tightly and ignored the pain. As the goddess's speed increased her heads moved back and forth in faster tempo as did the kirtle of snakes. The hissing was deafening.

Straight ahead to the valley wall he went, and then south to the temple. The priests would be finishing the morning service and this would be a good time to find them all together. He slowed Coatlicue as the pyramid came into sight, and the hissing diminished. Then, at a steady walking pace, he brought her around the steps of the pyramid and into their midst.

It was a frozen, heart-stopping moment. There was a sharp crash as the obsidian knife fell from Itzcoatl's hand as the first priest swayed with shock. The others were rigid, and the only motion was the incessant weaving of the snakes' heads. The priests turned faces, dumb with disbelief, upon the goddess and her rider, their eyes wide, the pupils contracted to dots.

"You have sinned!" Chimal screamed at them, waving the laser gun. It was doubtful if they even recognized him in his clothes the color of blood, perched high above them. "Coatlicue will have her vengeance. To the village of Quilapa, now—go. *Run!*"

The goddess started toward them, hissing outrageously, and they needed no more urging. They turned and fled and the snake-headed monster was at their heels. As they came to the village the first people appeared, stunned, all of them, by this frightening appearance and the unbelievable scene. Chimal gave them no time to gather their wits as he shouted orders at them to go on to Zaachila.

Chimal slowed the goddess as they came between the houses and the priests mingled with the crowd that poured out in a terrified wave. He did not permit them to stop, but scourged their flanks back and forth like a demonic herd. Women, children, babies—all of them—fled before him to the river and across. The first ones were already in Zaachila and the warning was given. Before he reached there the entire village was in flight from him.

"To the swamp!" he roared as they trampled through fields of corn stubble and fled between the rows of

137

maguey. "To the wall, to the cleft, to see what I will show you there!"

In blind panic they fled and he harried behind them. The palisade of the valley wall was ahead and the end was in sight. In a few minutes they would be in the tunnel and that would be the beginning of the end of the life they had known. Chimal laughed and shouted, tears streaming down his face. The end, the end . . .

A growing rumble, like distant thunder sounded ahead, and from the canyon wall a cloud of dust rolled out. The crowd slowed and stopped, milling about, not knowing which danger to flee from, then moved aside fearfully as Coatlicue plunged into their midst. Cold fear clutched hard at Chimal's chest as he rode toward the cleft in the towering walls.

He was afraid to admit what might have happened, dared not admit it to himself. He was close, too close to the end in every way for anything to go wrong now. Up the trail Coatlicue ran, and into the opening in the cliff.

To stop, dead, before the barrier of broken rock that sealed it from side to side.

A piece of rock clattered down the heap and then there was silence. The dust settled slowly. There was no trace of the stone doorway or of the opening to the caverns beyond, only the great heap of broken rock that covered the spot where it once had existed.

And then the darkness came. Clouds blew up, so suddenly that before the first thunderheads were even noticed the sky was covered with them. And even before they hid the sun, the sun itself dimmed and darkened and a cold wind raced the length of the valley. The people, huddled together, moaned in agony at the tragedy that befell them. Were the gods warring on Earth? What was happening? Was it the end?

Then the rain fell, adding to the darkness, and there was hail mixed with the freezing drops. The villagers broke and ran. Chimal fought the obscuring depression of defeat from his thoughts and turned Coatlicue to follow them. The fight wasn't over yet. Another way out could be found, Coatlicue would force the villagers to help him, their fear of her presence could not be washed away rain and darkness.

Halfway about the goddess stopped, rigid. The sn

138

were frozen in the endless coiling and their voices cut off short. For a second she leaned forward onto a partly raised foot, then came to rest. All the power had been cut off and the control box was useless. Chimal let it drop from his hand, then slowly and painfully slid down the wet and slippery metal back to the muddy ground.

He realized that the laser rifle was still in his hand; he pointed it at the rock barrier in a futile gesture of hatred and pulled hard on the trigger. But even this weak protest was denied him: the rain had penetrated its mechanism and it would not fire. He hurled it away from him.

The rain poured down and it was darker than the darkest night.

6

Chimal found himself sitting on the bank of the river, the roar of the water flooding by invisibly before him. His head rested on his knees and his right side, leg and arm, should do it soon before it became too deep. There was water sounded high and if he were going to cross he should do it soon before it became too deep. There was really no reason to cross, he would be just as dead on the outer side as he would be here, but Quilapa was over there and that was his village.

But when he tried to rise, to push himself to his feet, he found that he was frozen in the hunched position. The water had shorted out his eskoskeleton and it would permit only limited movements. With an effort he freed one arm, then released all the other fastenings. When he finally rose he left it behind like a discarded husk of a former life, perpetually crouching in obeisance by the water's edge. When he stepped into the river it came to his knees, then up to his waist before he was halfway across. He had to feel for each foothold carefully, leaning his weight against the current all of the time. If he were swept away now he knew that he would not be strong enough to swim to safety.

Step by step he went forward, the water tugging relentlessly at him: it would be so easy to give in and let it carry him away from everything. For some reason he found the idea distasteful—a sudden memory of the Air Tender hanging by his neck—and he rejected it and went on. The water was only to his thighs now, then below his knees again. He was across. Before climbing out he bent and filled his cupped hands and drank from them, many times. He was thirsty and in spite of the rain and the cold his skin was hot. His wounds did not bear thinking about.

Was there nowhere to go? Was it all over, forever? Chimal stood there, swaying in the darkness, his face up to the rain. Perhaps there really was a Great Designer who watched and thwarted him at every turning. No, that couldn't be true. He would not give in to a greater superstition now that he had discarded all his smaller ones. This world had been designed by men, built by men; he had read their proud reports and understood their thinking. He even knew the name of the one they called the Great Designer and knew the reasons why He had done all this. They were written in the books and could be read two ways.

Chimal knew that he had failed because of chance —and ignorance. It was luck that he had managed to come this far. A man was not made whole in a few short months. He had the knowledge of a man, perhaps. He had learnt so much and so quickly, but he still thought like a villager. Lash out. Run. Fight. Die. If only he could have done better.

If only he could have led his people through that painted hall and down the golden corridor to the stars.

And with this thought, this vision, came the first tiny inkling of hope.

Chimal walked on. He was again alone in the valley, and when the rains ceased and the sun came out the hunt would once more be on for him. How tenderly the priests would keep him alive for the tortures that they would invent and dwell upon. They who taught fear had felt fear, had run, craven. Their revenge would be exacting.

They would not have him. Once before, in absolute ignorance he had escaped the valley—he would do it again. Now he knew what lay behind the rock wall, wher the entrances were and what they led to. There had to be way to reach one of them. Ahead, on the top of the cl' was the entrance near which he had hidden his food water. If he could reach it he could rest and hide, make plans.

Yet even as he thought of it he knew that it was impossible. He had never been able to climb the valley walls when in perfect health and possessed of all his strength. It had been cunningly designed everywhere to prevent anyone from escaping in that manner. Even the vulture's ledge, far beneath the canyon's rim, would have been impossible to reach had not some chance accident broken a gap in the overhanging lip of rock.

In the darkness he stopped and laughed, until it turned into a fit of coughing.

That was the way. That might be the way out. Now he had a purpose and, in spite of the pain, he moved forward steadily in the streaming downpour. By the time he reached the valley wall the rain had lessened to a steady drizzle and the sky was lighter. The gods had made their point; they were still in command. They would gain nothing by flooding the valley.

Only they weren't gods, they were men. Fallible and stupid men whose work was finished even if they did not know it.

Through the falling rain he could make out the dark bulk of the pyramid as he passed it, but it was silent there and nothing moved. If the priests had returned they were now locked in their deepest chambers. He smiled and rubbed his knuckles across his mouth. Well, if he had done nothing else he had given them a fright they would never forget, oh yes he had. Perhaps this made up, in a very small way, for what they had done to his mother. These arrogant, strutting bullies would never again have the assurance that they were the final law among men.

When Chimal reached the spot below the ledge he stopped to rest. The rain had ceased but the valley was still swathed in a sea of damp fog. His left side was on fire and when he touched it his hand came away red with blood. Too bad. It was not going to stop him. This climb had to be made while vision was still obscured, so either the villagers nor the watching observers could see m. The pickups in the sky above would be useless now, t there might be others nearby that would be able to see . Certainly things would be upset now among the hmen, and the sooner he moved the better his chances

141

would be of doing it unseen. But he was so tired. He stood and placed his hands against the rock.

The only memory of the climb he had was one of pain. Red agony that fogged his vision and made it almost impossible to see. His fingers had to seek out grips on their own and his toes scuffled blindly for a place to rest. Perhaps he went up the same way he had used when he had climbed it as a boy: he could not be sure. The pain went on and on and the rock was slippery, with water or blood he could not tell. When he finally pulled himself over the rock lip onto the ledge he could not stand, could barely move. Pushing with his legs he slid his body through the wet filth on the ledge to the back of the shallow cave, beside the door. He would have to find a hiding place to one side, where he could not be seen through the concealed peephole, yet close enough to attack anyone who came. Crawling over he propped his back against the rock.

If they did not come soon it was all over. The climb had taxed him beyond his strength and he could barely stay conscious sitting there. Yet he must. He must be awake and alert and attack the next time the door was opened to feed the vultures. Then he must enter, attack, win. But he was so tired. Surely no one would come now, not until normal events were restored in the valley. Perhaps if he slept now he would be rested when the door did open. That would surely be some hours, perhaps a day more at least.

Yet, even as he was thinking this, there was a motion of air as the entrance in the rock swung up and out.

The suddenness of the happening, the gray weight of his fatigue, were too much for him. He could only gape as Watchman Steel appeared in the opening.

"What has happened?" she asked. "You must tell me what has happened."

"How did you find me . . . your screen?"

"Yes. We saw strange things happening in the valley, we heard rumors. No one seems to know the details. You have been missing, then I heard you were somewhere in the valley. I kept searching all the pickups, until I found yo What is happening? Tell me, please. None of us know it is . . . terrible . . . ." Her face was blank with fr

142

there is no destroyer like disorder in a world of complete order.

"Just what do you know?" he asked her as she helped him inside, to the seat in the car. After she had closed the feeding door she took a small container from her belt and passed it to him.

"Tea," she said. "You always liked it." Then fear of the unknown possessed her again as she remembered. "I never saw you again. You showed me the stars and told me about them, and kept shouting that we had passed Proxima Centauri, that we had to go back. Then we returned to the place where we had weight and you left me. I never saw you again. That has been days, many days now, and there has been trouble. The Observer at services tells us that evil walks the corridors but will not tell us what it is. He will not answer questions about you—it is as though you never existed. There have been alarms, strange things happening, two people have collapsed and died. Four girls are in hospital, they cannot work and we are all on extra shifts. Nothing is right. When I saw you on the screens, back in the valley, I thought you might know. And you are hurt too!" She realized the last, gasping and shrinking away, as the blood seeped from his side onto the seat.

"That happened days ago. I've had treatments. But I have done it no good today. Is there any kind of medicine in your belt?"

"The first aid kit, we are required to have one." She took it out with trembling fingers and he opened it and read the list of the contents. ·

"Very good." He opened his clothing and she turned away, eyes averted. "Bandages here, antiseptics, some pain pills. All of this should help." Then, with sudden understanding, "I'll tell you when you can look again." She bit her lip and nodded agreement, eyes shut.

"It appears your Master Observer has committed a grave error by not telling you about what has happened." He would censor his own story, there were some things she had better not know, but he would at least tell her the basic truth. "What I told you when we looked at the stars was true. We have passed Proxima Centauri. I know that ecause I found the navigation machines which told me out it. If you doubt it I can take you there and they will you too. I went to the Master Observer with my in-

143

formation and he did not deny it. If we turn now we can be at Proxima Centauri within 50 years, the goal of the Great Designer. But many years ago the Master Observer and others went against the Great Designer. I can prove this too with the log in the Master Observer's own quarters, the evidence of the men who decided this, and also decided to tell none of the others of you of this decision. Do you understand what I have told you so far?"

"I think I do." She spoke in an almost inaudible voice. "But it is all so terrible. Why should they do a thing like that? Not obeying the will of the Great Designer."

"Because they were wicked and selfish men, even if they were observers. And the observers now are no better. They are concealing the knowledge again. They will not permit me to reveal it. They have planned to send me away from here forever. Now—will you help me to right this wong?"

Once more the girl was far beyond her depth, floundering in concepts and responsibilities she was not equipped to handle. In her ordered life there was only obedience, never decision. She could not force herself to conclusions now. Perhaps the decision to run to him, to question him, had been the only act of free will she had ever accomplished in her entire lengthened, yet stunted, lifetime.

"I don't know what to do? I don't want to do anything. I don't know . . ."

"I know," he said, closing up his clothing and wiping his fingers on the cloth. He reached out and took her chin in his hand and turned her great empty eyes to him. "The Master Observer is the one who must decide, since that is his function in life. He will tell you whether I am right or wrong and what is to be done. Let us go to the Master Observer."

"Yes, let us go." She almost sighed with relief with the removal of the burden of responsibility. Her world was ordered again and the one whose appointed place in life was to decide, would decide. Already she was forgetting the confused events of the past days: they just did not fit into her regularized existence.

Chimal huddled low in the car so his soiled clothing would not be seen, but the effort was hardly necessary There were no casual walkers in the tunnels. Everyon must be manning the important stations—or w

144

physically unable to help. This hidden world was in as much of storm of change as the valley outside. With more change on the way, hopefully, Chimal thought as he eased himself from the car at the tunnel entrance nearest to the Master Observer's quarters. The halls were empty.

The oberver's quarters were empty too. Chimal went in, searched them, then dropped full length onto the bed.

"He'll be back soon. The best thing we can do is to wait here for him." There was little else, physically, that he could do at this time. The pain drugs made him sleepy and he dared not take any more of them. Watchman Steel sat in a chair, her hands folded on her lap, waiting patiently for the word of instruction that would strip away her problems. Chimal dozed, and woke with a start, then dozed again. The bedding and the warmth of the room dried his clothing and the worst of the pain ebbed away. His eyes closed and, in spite of himself, he slept.

The hand on his shoulder pulled him from the deep pit of sleep that he did not want to leave. Only when memory returned did he fight against it and force his eyelids open.

"There are voices outside," the girl said. "He is coming back. It is not seemly to be found here, lying like this."

Not seemly. Not safe. He would not be gassed and taken again. Yet it took every bit of will and energy he had remaining to pull himself erect, to stand, to lean on the girl and direct her to the far side of the room.

"We'll wait here in silence," he said, as the door opened.

"Do not call me until the machine is up, then," the Master Observer said. "I am tired and these days have taken years from my life. I must rest. Maintain the fog in the northern end of the valley in case someone might see. When the derrick is rigged one of you will ride it down to attach the cables. Do that yourselves. I must rest."

He closed the door and Chimal reached out and put both hands over his mouth.

7

The old man did not struggle. His hands fluttered limply for a moment and he rolled his eyes upward to look into Chimal's face, but otherwise he made no protest. Though he swayed with the effort, Chimal held the Master Observer until he was sure the men outside had gone, then released him and pointed to a chair.

"Sit," he commanded. "We shall all sit down because I can no longer stand." He dropped heavily into the nearest chair and the other two, almost docilely, obeyed his order. The girl was waiting for instruction: the old man was almost destroyed by the events of the preceding days.

"Look at what you have done," the Master Observer said hoarsely. "At the evils committed, the damage, the deaths. Now what greater evil do you plan . . ."

"Hush," Chimal said, touching his finger to his lips. He felt drained of everything vital, even of hatred at this moment, and his calmness quieted the others. The Master Observer mumbled into silence. He had not used his depilatory cream so there was gray stubble on his cheeks, as well as pockets of darkness under his eyes.

"Listen carefully and understand," Chimal began, in a voice so quiet that they had to strain to hear. "Everything has changed. The valley will never be the same again, you have to realize that. The Aztecs have seen me, mounted upon a goddess, have found out that everything is not as they always thought it was. Coatlicue may never walk again to enforce the taboo. Children will be born of parents of different villages, they will be Arrivers—but will not have an arrival. And your people here, what of them? They know that something is terribly wrong, yet they do not know what. You must tell them. You must do the only thing possible, and that is to turn the ship."

"Never!" Anger pulled the old man upright, and the eskosleleton helped his gnarled fingers to curl into fists. "The decision has been made and it cannot be changed."

"What decision is that?"

"The planets of Proxima Centauri were unsuitable. told you that. It is too late to return. We go on."

146

"Then we have passed Proxima Centauri . . . ?"

The Master Observer opened his mouth—then clamped it shut again as he realized the trap he had fallen into. Fatigue had betrayed him. He glared at Chimal, then at the girl.

"Go on," Chimal told him. "Finish what you were going to say. That you and other observers have worked against the Great Designer's plan and have turned us from our orbit. Tell this girl so she may tell the others."

"This is none of your affair," the old man snapped at her. "Leave and do not discuss what you have heard here."

"Stay," Chimal said, pressing her back into her seat as she half rose at the order. "There is more truth to come. And perhaps after while the observer will realize that he wants you here where you cannot tell the others what you know. Then later he will think of a way to kill you or to send you off into space. He must keep his guilty secret because if he is found out he is destroyed. Turn the ship, old man, and do one good thing with your life."

Surprise was gone and the Master Observer had control of himself again. He touched his deus and bowed his head. "I have finally understood what you are. You are to evil as the Great Designer is to good. You have come to destroy and you shall not succeed. What you are . . ."

"Not good enough," Chimal broke in. "It is too late to call names or settle this by insult. I give you facts, and I ask you to dare deny them. Watch him closely, Steel, and listen to his answers. I give you first the statement that we are no longer on the way to Proxima Centauri. Is that fact?"

The old man closed his eyes and did not answer, then crouched in his chair in fear as Chimal sprang to his feet. But Chimal went by him and pulled the red-bound log from the rack and let it fall open. "Here is the fact, the decision that you and the others made. Shall I let the girl read it?"

"I do not deny it. This was a wise decision made for the good of all. The watchman will understand. She, and all he others will obey, whether they are told or not."

"Yes, you're probably right," Chimal said, wearily, rling the book aside and dropping back into his chair. nd that is the biggest crime of all. No not yours, His.

The most evil one, the one you call the Great Designer"

"Blasphemy," the Master Observer croaked, and even Watchman Steel shrank back from the awfulness of Chimal's words.

"No, just truth. The books told me that there are things called nations on Earth. They seem to be large groups of people, though not all of the people on Earth. It is hard to tell exactly why these nations exist or what their purpose is, but that is not important. What is important is that one of these nations was led by the man we now call the Great Designer. You can read his name, the name of the country, they are meaningless to us. His power was so great he built a memorial to himself greater than any ever constructed before. In his writings he says how the thing he does is greater than the pyramids or anything that came before. He says that pyramids are great structures, but that his structure is greater—an entire world. This world. In detail he writes how it was designed and made and sent on its way and he is very proud of it. Yet what he is really proud of is the people who live in this world, who will go out to the stars and carry human life in his name. Don't you see why he feels that way? He has created an entire race to worship his image. He has made himself God."

"He is God," the Master Observer said, and Watchman Steel nodded agreement and touched her deus.

"Not God, or even a black god of evil, though he deserves that name. Just a man. A frightful man. The books talk of the wonders of the Aztecs he created to carry out his mission, their artificially induced weakness of mind and docility. This is no wonder—but a crime. Children were born, from the finest people in the land, and they were stunted before birth. They were taught superstitious nonsense and bundled off into this prison of rock to die without hope. And, even worse, to raise their children in their own imbecilic image for generation after generation of blunted, wasted lives. You know that, don't you?"

"It was His will," the old man answered, untroubled.

"Yes it was, and it doesn't bother you at all because you are the leader of the jailers who imprison this race, and you wish to continue the imprisonment forever Poor fool. Did you ever think where you and your peopl came from? Is it chance that you are all so faithful to yo" trust and so willing to serve? Don't you realize that you were *made* in the same way the Aztecs were made? That after finding the ancient Aztecs as a model society for the valley dwellers, this monster looked for a group to do the necessary housekeeping for the centuries-long voyage. He found it in the mysticism and monasticism that has always been a nasty side path taken by the human race. Hermits wallowing in filth in caves, others staring into the sun for a lifetime of holy blindness, orders that withdrew from the world and sealed themselves away for lives of sacred misery. Faith replacing thinking and ritual replacing intelligence. This man examined all the cults and took the worst he could find to build the life you lead. You worship pain, and hate love and natural motherhood. You are smug with the years of your long lives and look down upon the short-lived Aztecs as lower animals. Don't you realize the ritualized waste of your empty lives? Don't you understand that your intelligence has also been dimmed and diminished so that none of you will question the things you have to do? Can you not see that you are just as much condemned prisoners as the people in the valley?"

Exhausted, Chimal dropped back in his chair, looking from the cold face of hatred to the empty face of incomprehension. No, they had no idea what he was talking about. There was no one, in the valley or out, whom he could talk to, communicate with, and a cold loneliness settled on him.

"No, you cannot see," he said, with weary resignation. "The Great Designer has designed too well."

At his words their fingers automatically went to their deuses and he was too tired to do more than sigh.

"Watchman Steel," he ordered, "there is food and drink over there. Bring them to me." She hurried to his bidding. He ate slowly, washing the food down with the still-warm tea from the Thermos, while he planned what to do next.

The Master Observer's hand crept to the communicator at his waist and Chimal had to reach out and pull it from his belt. "Yours too," he told Watchman Steel, and did not bother to explain why he wanted it. She would obey in either case. He could expect no more help from anyone. From now on he was alone.

"There is none higher than you, is there, Master Observer?" he asked.

"All know that, except you."

"I know it too, you must realize that. And when the decision was made to change the orbit, the observers agreed but the final decision was made by the then Master Observer. Therefore you are the one who must know all of the details of this world, where the spaceships are and how to activate them, the nagivation and how it is done, and the schools and all the arrangements for the Day of Arrival, everything."

"Why do you ask me these things?"

"I'll make my meaning clear. There are many responsibilities here, far too many to be passed on by word of mouth from one Master Observer to the other. So there are charts that show all the tunnels and chambers and their contents, and there are breviaries for the schools and the spaceship. Why there must even be a breviary for that wonderful day of arrival when the valley is open—*where is it?*"

The last words were a demanding question and the old man started and his eyes jumped to the wall, then instantly away. Chimal turned to look up at the red-lacquered cabinet that hung there, in front of which a light always burned. He had noticed it before but never thought consciously about it.

When he rose to go to it the Master Observer attacked him, his aged hands and the rods of his eskoskeleton striking Chimal about the head and shoulders. Finally, he had understood what Chimal had in mind. The struggle was brief. Chimal prisoned the old man's hands, clasping them together behind his back. Then he remembered the failure of his own eskoskeleton and threw the power switch on the Master Observer's harness. The motors died and the joints locked, holding the man captive. Chimal picked him up gently and laid him on his side on the bed.

"Watchman Steel, duty," the old man ordered, though his voice quavered. "Stop him. Kill him. I order you to do this."

Unable to understand more than a fraction of what had occurred the girl stood, wavering helplessly between them.

"Don't worry," Chimal told her. "Everything will be all right." Against her slight resistance he forced her back into the chair and disconnected her eskoskeleton too, tearing the power pack free. He tied her wrists together as well, with a cloth from the ablutory.

Only when they were both secured did he go to the cabinet on the wall and tug at its doors. They were locked. In a sudden temper he tore at it, pulling it bodily from the wall, ignoring the things the Master Observer was calling at him. The lock on the cabinet was more decorative than practical and the whole thing fell to pieces easily when he put it on the floor and stamped on it. He bent and picked a red-bound and gold decorated book from the wreckage.

"The Day of Arrival," he read, then opened it. "That day is now."

The basic instructions were simple enough, as were the instructions in all the breviaries. The machines would do the work, they had only to be activated. Chimal went over in his mind the course he would take, and hoped that he could walk that far. Pain and fatigue were closing in again and he could not fail now. The old man and the girl were both silent, too horrified by what he was doing to react. But this could change as soon as he left. He needed time. There were more cloths in the ablutory and he took them and sealed their mouths with them. If somone should pass they would not be able to give the alarm. He threw the communicators to the ground and broke them as well. He would not be stopped.

As he put his hand on the door he turned to face the wide, accusing eyes of the girl. "I'm right," he told her. "You'll see. There is much happiness ahead." Taking the breviary for the Day of Arrival, he opened the door and left.

The caverns were still amost empty of people which was good: he did not have the strength to make any detours. Halfway to his goal he passed two watchmen, both girls, coming off duty, but they only stared with frightened empty eyes as he passed. He was almost to the entrance to the hall when he heard shouting and looked back to see the red patch of an observer hurrying after him. Was this chance—or had the man been warned? In either case, all he could do was go on. It was a nightmare chase, something out of a dream. The watchman walked at the highest speed his eskoskeleton would allow, coming steadily on. Chimal was unrestricted, but wounded and exhausted. He ran ahead, slowed, hobbled on, while the observer, shouting hoarse threats, ground in pursuit like

151

some obscene mixture of man and machine. Then the door to the great chamber was ahead and Chimal pushed through it and closed it behind him, leaning his weight against it. His pursuer slammed into the other side.

There was no lock, but Chimal's weight kept the door closed against the other's hammering while he fought to catch his breath. When he opened the breviary his blood ran down the whiteness of the page. He looked at the diagram and the instructions again, then around the immensity of the painted chamber.

To his left was the wall of great boulders and massive rocks, the other side of the barrier that sealed the end of his valley. Far off to his right were the great portals. And halfway down this wall was the spot he must find.

He started toward it. Behind him the door burst open and the observer fell through, but Chimal did not look back. The man was down on his hands and knees and motors hummed as he struggled to rise. Chimal looked up at the paintings and found the correct one easily enough. Here was a man who stood out from the painted crowd of marchers, who stood away from them, bigger than them. Perhaps it was an image of the Great Designer himself: undoubtedly it was. Chimal looked into the depths of those nobly painted eyes and, if his mouth had not been so dry, he would have spat into the wide-browed perfection of the face. Instead he leaned forward, his hand making a red smear along the wall, until his fingers touched those of the painted image.

Something clicked sharply and a panel fell open, and there was a single large switch inside. Then the observer was upon Chimal as he clutched at it, and they fell together.

Their combined weight pulled it down.

8

Atototl was an old man, and perhaps because of this the priests in the temple considered him expendable. Then again, since he was the cacique of Quilapa he was a man of standing and people would listen when he brought back a report. And he could be expected to obey. But, whatever their reasons, they had commanded him to go forth and he had bowed his head in submission and done as they had ordered.

The storm had passed and even the fog had lifted. Were it not for the black memories of earlier events it could have been the late afternoon of almost any day. A day after a rain, of course, the ground was still damp underfoot and off to his right he could hear the water in the river, rushing high against the banks as it drained the sodden fields. The sun shone warmly and brought little curls of mist from the ground. Atototl came to the edge of the swamp and squatted on his heels and rested. Was the swamp bigger than when he had seen it last? It seemed to be, but surely it would have to be larger after all that rain. But it would get lower again, it always had before. This was nothing to be concerned about, yet he must remember to tell the priests about it.

What a frightening place the world had become. He would almost prefer to leave it and wander through the underworlds of death. First there had been the death of the first priest and the day that was a night. Then Chimal had gone, taken by Coatlicue the priests had said, and it certainly had seemed right. It must have been that way, but even Coatlicue had not been able to keep that spirit captive. It had returned with Coatlicue herself, riding her great back, garbed in blood and hideous, yet still bearing the face of Chimal. What could it all mean? And then the storm. It was all beyond him. A green blade of new grass grew at his feet and he reached down and broke it off, then chewed on it. He would have to go back soon to the priests and tell them what he had seen. The swamp was bigger, he must not forget that, and there was certainly no sign of Coatlicue.

He stood up and stretched his tired leg muscles, and as he did so he felt a distant rumbling. What was happening now? In terror he clutched his arms about himself, unable to run away while he stared at the waves that trembled the surface of the water before him. There was another rumble, louder this time, that he could feel in his feet, as though the entire world were shaking beneath him.

Then, with cracklings and grumblings the entire barrier of stone that sealed the mouth of the valley began to stir and slide. One great boulder moved downward, then another and another. Sinking into the solid ground, faster and faster, all of them moving, rushing down, crumbling and cracking and grinding together until they vanished from sight below. Then, as the valley opened up, the waters before him began to recede, rushing after the rock barrier, trickling and bubbling away in a thousand small cataracts, hurrying after the dam that had held it so long. Quickly the water ran, until a brown waste of mud, silvered with the flapping bodies of fish, stretched out where there had only been ponds and swamp just minutes before. Reaching out to the cliffs that were no longer a barrier but an exit from the valley, that framed *something* golden and glorious, filled with light and marching figures—Atototl spread his arms wide before the wonder of it all.

"It is the day of deliverance," he said, no longer afraid. "And all the strange things came before it. We are free. We shall leave the valley at last."

Hesitantly, he put one foot forward onto the still soft mud.

The booming of explosions was deafening inside the hall. As they started the observer fell away and cowered in panic on the floor. Chimal held to the great switch for support as the floor shook and the boulders stirred. This was the reason for the location of the carved reservoir below. Everything had been planned. The barrier that sealed the valley must stand on the stone just above th hollowed-out chamber. Now supports were being blow away and the rock weakened. The entire roof was falli away. With a final roar the last boulders tumbled do

154

ward, filling the reservoir below with their tops making a broken roadway out of the valley. Sunlight streamed in through the opening and fell upon the paintings for the first time.

Outside Chimal could see the valley with the mountains beyond and he knew that this time he had not failed.

This action was irreversible, the barrier was gone.

His people were free.

"Get up," he said to the observer who was groveling against the wall. He pushed at him with his toe. "Get up and look and try to understand. Your people are free too."

THE BEGINNING

1

Ah tlamiz noxochiuh ah tlamiz
   nocuic
In noconehua
Xexelihui ya moyahua

My flowers shall not die, my songs will
   yet be heard
They spread
Endlessly

Chimal pulled himself down the axis of rotation tunnel, grumbling when his left shoulder touched against one of the bars and the now familiar pain shot down his arm. The arm was getting more useless and painful all the time. He would have to get back to the surgical machines one of these days for another operation—or have the cursed thing taken off if they could do nothing more about it. If they had fixed it correctly in the first place this need not have happened. Not that he had done it much good bashing and battering with it. Still, he had done what had to be done at the time. He must make some time for the surgery, and soon.

The elevator lowered him back to the area of gravity and Matlal opened the door for him.

"On course," Chimal told the guard, handing him the books and records to carry. "The orbit correction is going through just as the computer said it would. We're cutting a great arc now, curving in space, though we can't feel it in here. This will take years. But we are now on the way to Proxima Centauri."

The man nodded, neither attempting nor desiring to un derstand what Chimal was talking about. It did not ma ter. Chimal was talking for his own benefit in any case: seemed to be doing a lot of that lately. He limped slo down the corridor and the Aztec followed him.

156

"How do the people like the new water that has been piped into the villages?" Chimal asked.

"It doesn't taste the same," Matlal said.

"Aside from the taste," Chimal said, trying not to lose his temper, "isn't it easier than carrying it the way you used to? And isn't there more food now, and the sick people are cured? What about that?"

"It's different. Sometimes it is . . . not right that things should be different."

Chimal didn't really expect any praise, not from a society as conservative as this. He would keep them healthy and well-fed in spite of themselves. For their children's sake, if not for theirs. He would keep the Aztec with him as a source of information, if for no other reason. There was no time for him to personally watch the valley people. He had taken Matlal, the strongest man in both villages, as a personal guard in the first days after the barrier had been opened. At that time he had no idea how the Watchers would act and he wanted someone to defend him in case of violence. Now there was no longer any need for protection, but he would keep him as an informant.

Not that he need have worried about violence. The Watchers had been as stunned by events as had the people in the valley. When the first Aztecs had pushed through the mud and over the broken rock they had been dazed and uncomprehending. The two groups met and passed without touching, unable at the moment to assimilate the others' presence. Discipline had been restored only when Chimal had found the Master Observer and had handed over the breviary of the Day of Arrival. Bound by discipline the old man had had no choice. He had taken it without looking at its donor, then turned away and issued the first order. The Day of Arrival had begun.

Discipline and order had pulled together the Watchers, and an unaccustomed vitality had penetrated their lives. Here, now, in their lifetimes, they were fulfilling the promise that generations had been trained for. If the observers regretted the termination of the time of watching the ordinary tenders and watchmen did not. They seemed, for the first time, to be almost wholly alive.

While the Master Observer ordered their operations as had been written. There were breviaries and rules for everything and they were obeyed. He was in charge and

Chimal never questioned it. Yet Chimal knew that his blood inerasably marked the pages of the breviary of the Day of Arrival that the old man carried. That was enough for him. He had done what had to be done.

As he passed the door of one of the classrooms Chimal looked in, at his people bent over the education machines. They had furrowed foreheads for the most part and probably understood very little of what they were watching. That did not matter; the machines were not for them. The best that could be expected was an alleviating of the absolute ignorance that they lived in. Easier lives, better conditions. They needed contentment and health as the parents of the next generation. The machines were for the children—they would know what use to put them to.

Further down were the children's quarters. Bare and empty now—but waiting. And the maternity wards, many of them bright and empty too, but it would not be too long until they were put to a good use. Give the Great Designer credit once again, there had been no protests when the booming voices in the hall had removed the taboo against intermarriage, had even said it was the only correct course. Everything had been worked out to the last, finest detail.

There was a motion inside and Chimal turned to look through the window at Watchman Steel sitting on a chair against the far wall.

"Go get some food, Matlal," he ordered, "I'll be down shortly. Put those things in my quarters first."

The man saluted, automatically raising his hand in the gesture of obeisance that he used to a priest, and left. Chimal went inside and sat down wearily across from the girl. He had been working hard, since the Master Observer had left him to his own devices with the navigation and the change of orbit. That was under automatic control now. Maybe he could take time for the surgeons, though it would probably mean some days in bed.

"How long must I keep coming here?" the girl asked, the familiar, wounded look still in her eyes.

"Never again, if you don't want to," he told her, too tired to argue. "Do you think I'm doing this for my sake?'

"I don't know."

"Then try and think. What possible pleasure could I •
158

from forcing you to look at pictures of babies, pregnant women, obstetric films?"

"I don't know. There are so many things that it is not possible to explain."

"And a lot that are explainable. You're a woman, and outside of your training and development, a normal woman. I want to, perhaps, it is hard to say exactly, give you a chance to *feel* like a woman. I think you have been cheated by life."

Her fists clenched. "I don't want to think like a woman. I am a watchman. That is my duty and my glory—and I do not wish to be anything else." The little spark of anger burned out as quickly as it had come. "Please let me go back to my work. Aren't there enough women among the valley people to make you happy? I know you think that I am not smart, that none of us are smart, but that is the way we are. Can't you leave us alone to do what we must do?"

Chimal looked at her, comprehending for the first time.

"I'm sorry," he said. "I have been trying to make you something you are not and preventing you from being something that you want to be. Because I changed I keep feeling that everyone else should want to change too. But what I am has been planned by the Great Designer just as well as what you are. With me, yes, desire to change and understand is the most important thing possible. I hold onto that, no matter what. It is as important to me, and as satisfying, as that thing—what was it—your mortification used to be you."

"As it *is* to me," she called out, standing and, in a moment of righteous strength opening her clothing to turn out the gray edge of fabric to him that circled her body. "I do penance for both of us."

"Yes, you do that," he said as she closed her clothing, trembling again at her audacity, and hurried out.

"We should all do penance for the thousands who died over the years to get us here. At least there is finally an end to all that."

Chimal looked at the rows of empty beds and bassinets, waiting, and realized not for the first time how completely alone he was. Well, that he could get used to, and it was not very different from the loneliness that he had always

159

known. And they would be coming along soon, the children.

Within a year there would be babies, and a few years later they would be talking. Chimal felt a sudden identification with those unborn children. He knew how they would look around at the world, wondering. He knew the eager questions that would be on their lips.

And this time there would be answers to those questions. The empty years of his childhood would never be repeated. The machines would answer their questions and so would he.

At that thought he smiled, peopling the empty room with the eager-eyed children of his mind. Yes, the children.

Patience, Chimal, in a few short years you will never be alone again.